I0592533

ALSO BY CHARLOTTE EASTER EARL

The Voiceless Scream

THE ARDUOUS CASE OF THE LOST PRINCESS

THE ARDUOUS CASE OF THE LOST PRINCESS

A HERCULES POTATO ADVENTURE

CHARLOTTE EASTER EARL

Copyright ©2018 by Charlotte Easter Earl

All rights reserved. Published in the United States by Middlemarch Press

Middlemarch Press is a registered Trademark.

Library of Congress Control Number: 2018903402

ISBN 978-0-692-07981-2

1. Potato, Hercules (Fictitious Character)—Fiction.2. Little Marchmain (Imaginary House)—Fiction.3. Canine detective—Dale-on-Tweedy-Down—Fiction.4. Shady Tabby Cats—Fiction.5. Heroes and Dogs—Fiction. 6. Dale-on-Tweedy-Down (Imaginary Village)—Fiction.

Middlemarch Press, Literature Lives Here
Arlington, Virginia

For Peter, a.k.a. Mr. Easter Earl.

THE ARDUOUS CASE OF THE LOST PRINCESS

Dear Reader,

Hercules Potato, Belgian Griffon and famed detective, comes from a country called Belgium. While French is his native language, he is a bilingual dog, so he speaks English throughout this story. However, because English is his second language, you will discover his speech is delightfully peppered with French expressions, particularly if he becomes agitated or excited over events. If you do not understand the French words he sometimes uses, I urge you not to fret about it. These foreign words neither impact the meaning of the English words nor the plot of the story, and you may even find you understand exactly what they mean from the context in which Hercules Potato speaks them.

If you are a bit like me, and you enjoy learning the words of other languages, I include at the back of this book a complete list and translation of the French words and phrases that leap from the mouth of Hercules Potato throughout this story. This is offered purely for your enjoyment and amusement. Fear not, there is to be no test at the end of anything here concerned.

Your Affectionate Author,

C. E. Earl,

10 March, 2018

TABLE OF CONTENTS

～

≈

No actual chickens were harmed in the writing of this story.

(I regret the same is not able to be said of certain of the fish.)

(As for the rats, well...)

≈

CHAPTER I

THE FAMED DETECTIVE AT HOME

Little Marchmain

*I*n a place you might not know, in a county you have possibly never visited, there is a village nestled against the foot of a high hill and resting upon the hand of a sprawling valley. It is a lovely spread of peaceful life, rich with many trees and lanes and ponds. Pleasure is ever ready to appear in the form of long walks, in the notable smells of mostly pleasing descriptions, and in the finding of many excellent sticks.

If you enter from the far edge of the valley, where the village of Dale-on-Tweedy-Down begins, and if you take the second lane off of the High Street as it sweeps you along, you will pass beneath many maples and oaks and elms. Then, coming to the fifth house on the left, the one with the tree swing in the front garden, you will see a plaque reading, "Little Marchmain," and you will find a wooden gate parting the length of a Portuguese laurel hedge.

If you enter beyond this gate and allow the reclaimed stone pathway to guide you through a particularly charming front garden, you will have arrived at the home of Hercules Potato, Belgian Griffon and famed detective. Just at present, you are advised against ringing the bell, for it is as yet in the wee small hours before sunrise, and all within are deep in sleep. While dawn makes its approach towards this day in late spring, the scene inside the house, posed as it is in stillness, is nonetheless worth knowing about.

Sometime during the night, one Pookie Shams, mixed poodle terrier and very good at rats, jumped onto the bed of a slumbering hero and settled himself there in perfect comfort. His had been an act of shameless disregard for house rules. Dogs are not allowed on heroes' beds in Little Marchmain, but as his infraction took place under cover of darkness, no authority stepped in to admonish him.

In this bed slept the petite hero Montcy Thistlewait, six years old and clever to boot. On the opposite side of the second floor passage, slept the petite hero Lewis Thistlewait, ten years old and not normally one to miss the boat. Deep in his REM cycle, however, he was unaware he slumbered without the canine solidarity currently enjoyed by his sister.

In the largest bedroom, slept the two grand heroes Thistlewait, parents and chief presiders over all things passing within the

2

jurisdiction of the house called Little Marchmain. The grand hero Gavin, lord and master of the front garden, was in this moment, fondly dreaming of accepting the village summer prize in the Best & Beautiful Garden contest. His nemesis, Sir Wordsworth Plumm, glowered at his success from the dream's hazy, peripheral edge.

The grand hero Gwendolyn, dearly loved by all the house inmates, despite her being rather over fond of rules, also dreamed on. Her dream saw her proudly presenting her renowned White Room to a photographer and a writer, sent by *Ville & Village Magazine* to capture it for a front cover spread.

Downstairs, snuffling snores rose up from the kitchen cushion of Hercules Potato, Belgian Griffon and famed detective, as he dreamed his way hot on the trail of a rat. Deep in subconscious excitement, spasmodic and agitated jerks animated his otherwise resting limbs. One is never at one's most prestigious appearance while asleep, and it would pain this particular dog terribly to know the picture just described is the first opportunity given to the public to observe him. In deference to his strong feelings on matters of personal appearance and decorum, a more in depth description of the famed detective and his antecedents must here be presented.

By accident of fortune, Hercules Potato was not a large dog. He was not even a medium-sized dog. He was, in all frankness, a small dog. Put rather more bluntly, he was a toy-sized dog, but he always thought it impolite whenever he heard himself spoken of as such. When sitting on his haunches, his head measured, at most, thirty-five centimeters from the ground. To anyone impertinent enough to call him, "a tiny dog," he would always be quick to point out he in fact enjoyed a larger stature than most teacup poodles of his acquaintance. Life was not without its consolations.

The fur at his brief crown began as black and kept dark around his small ears, which flapped curtly forward. An exceptional moustache grew under his markedly flat nose, which nature placed nearly in line with his almond shaped, black eyes. This moustache, in which he prided himself, was of a light brown colour. It blended into a distinguished, brownish black beard, growing out around his tiny mouth and helping to obscure his rather weak jaw line—his least favourite attribute. Most of the rest of his fur grew out black again around his short, thick body, but flashes of brown highlights appeared on his chest, and his four paws wore spat-like light brown fur.

He bore himself along by a dashingly smart carriage, and his meticulous grooming habits ensured others rarely ever saw him out of form. "One may not have the control of one's height," he could often be heard to say, "but this is not the excuse allowable for the bad grooming."

The grand hero Gavin first brought the two-year-old dog home after a business trip to Belgium. The petite hero Lewis, then five years old, took charge of his naming ceremony. The lad had lately been absorbed in tales from Greek mythology, and he at first proposed to name the small dog after the strong and mighty son of god and mortal, Hercules.

The grand hero Gavin had said, "I'm not sure it quite fits in this instance, my boy. This one here is more like a potato than anything to do with a Greek god. What's more, I rather doubt he will ever be up to slaying a Nemean lion or any lion at all if it comes to it."

The petite hero Lewis quite took his father's point and said, "Then we can call him Hercules Potato."

"I say, that is rather better, my boy. Hercules Potato it shall be, and em' do let's train him straightaway about the gods frowning on any digging or tearing about in the front garden."

Thus concluded the solemnity of the naming ceremony, and, true to the grand hero Gavin's prediction, Hercules Potato did not turn out to be good at Nemean lions. Neither, as it also turned out, was he good at rats.

Two centuries ago, heroes prized and praised the Belgian Griffon breed because these small dogs were especially good at

Out tumbled a small mass of white disheveled fur. The petite hero Montcy squealed with pleasure. The petite hero Lewis shouted, "Hooray, a new puppy." The grand heroes Gavin and Gwendolyn beamed lovingly over the entire brood. Hercules Potato scowled.

The little white dog went in all directions at the same time, bursting with outsized excitement and zeal to make his figurative mark upon the fellowship. Quite soon, he made his literal mark upon the kitchen floor. This sent the entire group outside to the back garden. There, on a tuft of grass near some shrubbery, they instructed the new puppy in his first teachable moment regarding the household's sanitary expectations of him.

Later, the grand hero Gavin said, "I say, how bout we have the ole naming ceremony, eh my Montcy? What are your thoughts about what to call your birthday puppy?"

She hesitated then said, "I don't know, maybe . . ." She thought a bit more. As it happened, her other birthday gift had been her very first grown-up sized bed, and she fancied the pretty, ruffled, ivory pillow sham topping the bright new set-up. "I think he looks like a pillow sham."

"I think he looks like a pook," said the petite hero Lewis, who had lately been absorbed by an old book about farming. Its chapter on haystacks interested him the most, and from it he had learned that farmers used to refer to heaps of hay and high piles of corn as 'pooks.' Of course, his suggestion for the puppy's name sprang more from his desire to run around shouting "Pook, Pook," than it did from any actual resemblance in the new puppy to an 18th century haystack.

"*Moi*, I think this one, he looks just like the arsenic crystal," said Hercules Potato, who had only the week before been involved in a case involving arsenic and the scent of old lace. Of course, no one heard him state his opinion.

"Splendid, my darlings," said the grand hero Gwendolyn, "which one should we choose?"

"Pookie," proclaimed the petite hero Lewis.

"Pillow Shams," proclaimed the petite hero Montcy.

"*Cristal d'Arsenic,*" proclaimed Hercules Potato, though no one heard him say it.

"Why don't we call him Pookie Shams," said the petite hero Montcy. Her compromise won the day, and with the naming ceremony concluded, the heroes all started in on the birthday cake. Hercules Potato groaned inwardly and sought solace on his kitchen cushion.

The following weeks and months proved a difficult transition for Hercules Potato. To his friend the Colonel, an Airedale who lived across the lane and whom we shall hear more from later, Hercules Potato said, "Pookie Shams, he is a dog so much given to vicissitude. He cannot make up his mind. If he one minute begins to go in search of the buried bone, the next minute he is stopping to chew the shoes. If he starts out to answer the call of nature, his bladder brimming cannot trust him to proceed to the crucial business, because meantime, a bicycle, it invites him to chase after it. *Non,* there is nothing about this dog the scents and the logic can guide."

Despite his lack of a flexible or deep intellect, Pookie Shams, it just unhappily turned out, was very good at the one thing zapping at Hercules Potato's rawest nerve — Pookie Shams was good at rats. One afternoon, when sunshine and sweet breezes were especially delighting the village of Dale-on-Tweedy-Down, Hercules Potato was circling round a tree in the front garden at Little Marchmain. It was the friendly tree with the swing hanging from one of its sturdy branches. The swing that gave the petite heroes so much enjoyment, however much it gave the grand hero Gavin heartburn whenever their feet landed too near the hostas gracefully encircling said tree.

Hercules Potato completed his round, and he was just about to compliment the tree by raising his leg to it, when he froze. He heard it - he knew he heard it. He thrust his head forward and prepared his nostrils for the intake of the crucial information. He drew in a long and studied stream of air. His nasal passages sent back to him a detailed report of green grass, multiple variations of tree bark, rustling leaves, inviting dirt, out-of-reach birds, irritating squirrels, and the nearby presence of Pookie Shams. The report made no mention of a rat of any description.

He crumpled down on the ground in a heap of disappointment just as Pookie Shams burst through the Portuguese laurel. His tail wagging, he carried in his mouth a rat of substantial size. Hercules Potato felt the ice of a thousand winters freeze instantly within his soul. Pookie Shams trotted up to him and dropped the dead rat at the famed detective's front paws. He wagged his tail again, panted enthusiastically, glowed with pride, and showed by all of these glad tidings how it pleased him beyond measure to gift his capture to his best friend, Hercules Potato. He licked him on his ear, and then bounded off to chase the petite hero Lewis around back of the house. Hercules Potato gazed down at the dead rat and sniffed it. Nothing. He smelled absolutely nothing.

∾

THE WIDER PUBLIC is likely to consider it most appropriate that its first glimpse of Hercules Potato came at a moment whilst he slept on in the earnest dream of catching a rat. Though as has been noted, the dog concerned would quite naturally take an altogether different view of the matter if he knew about it. The dream chase, however, ended no better for the sleeping, famed detective than it might have done had he been fully awake.

The rat's tail just disappeared round a flickering corner when an alarm clock rang out upstairs. An unseen hand silenced it in a moment, and the Belgian Griffon, chased on after his prey. As he flew round the bend, the rat came into full view. *"Finalement,"* cried the dog in his dream. The alarm went off again, and this time begrudging shuffles could be heard moving overhead. Hercules Potato was in mid-spring—his front paws just closing in upon the fleeing rat—when the kitchen flooded with light and his dream evaporated.

He lay blinking for a moment, wincing at the yip, yip, yipping of Pookie Shams, who might have been pouring into a pep rally rather than arriving at breakfast. Hercules Potato closed his eyes again and briefly lamented the narrow escape of his rat. Then he too sprang up from his bed in order to do his bit to ensure the breakfast routine went off without a hitch.

Cereal began filling into bowls, and happily for the dogs concerned, spilling onto the floor. The phone rang; drawers slammed; footsteps went back and forth, in and out of rooms, and overhead. The pipes sang as hot water shot through them, and later, a blow dryer joined in the cacophony. The grand hero Gavin, true to form, did not forget the most important aspect of the morning program. "Time for walkies, fellows," he said, as he clicked their leads onto their collar hooks.

Once out the back door, the two dogs offered proper homage to the section of shrubbery the grand hero Gavin always encouraged them to make use of for that purpose. This done, the trio headed around to the front garden, where he said with evident pride in his voice, "Ah yes, it does look well, doesn't it, fellows."

Pookie Shams sniffed at a grouping of Hyacinth growing along the reclaimed stone pathway, while Hercules Potato, distracted at keeping a close eye on his careless companion, tripped head long over a loose stone. For a small dog, it wasn't far to go to meet the ground, and he reclaimed all fours having escaped injury. The grand hero Gavin stooped down to examine him, and said, "Sorry, Hercules Potato, I'll need to fix this stone over the weekend, but you are none the worse for taking a tumble. Good boy."

He picked up the stone and put it back into place while Hercules Potato ran a paw through his beard and moustache so as to ensure they had not been ruffled in his misadventure.

"Hullo, what's this?" asked the grand hero Gavin. For, in stooping to replace the stone in the garden path, his weigela border shrub caught his eye. Hercules Potato sniffed dutifully at his hero's feet and ankles. The grand hero's scent had transformed from his well-recognised, happy hero aroma, to a much lesser known redolence of unhappy hero.

"It's drooping. That won't do at all. It must not be getting enough water. I need to see to this sharpish. Wait here, fellows."

He disappeared round the house, and reappeared carrying a hosepipe. As he walked, he aimed its spray at parts of the grass and at the busy Lizzies potted along the front porch and hanging above it. Reaching his parched weigela, he gave it a generous spray, before once again disappearing behind the house. Reappearing without the hosepipe and drying his hands on his trousers, he returned to take up the dogs' leads.

Hercules Potato sniffed at his hero's ankles and felt relief to once again smell the beloved scent of his hero in a state of gladsome happiness. "Nothing to worry about, fellows, its little morning spray will soon put our weigela right again," and opening the gate he said, "Good thing you tripped on that stone, Hercules Potato, or I might not have seen it this morning. Thirsty plants don't bear delay."

As they passed into the lane, Hercules Potato glanced back at the weigela and thought it happier for having taken its drink of water. Then he turned his attention to the delights of the morning walk. The air still felt slightly chilly, the sun not yet having had enough time to thoroughly do its work. As Hercules Potato trotted next to Pookie Shams, he breathed in deep draughts of the scents so wonderful in morning time.

Later in the afternoon, these would fade and give way to others scents, but for now, smells like the slug slime trailing along the dewy earth rose up in prominent strength. As he knew of his hero Gavin's acute dislike of slugs, he hoped none had found their way into the front garden. Above him, the martins' chirped and warbled. Below, he sniffed appreciatively at the cow manure spread there to encourage the newly budding flowers to do their best.

Here and there, the grand hero Gavin would remark, "The grass over there does need a spot of fertiliser," or, "Poor Mrs. Blevins, with all those trees crowding out the sunlight, she really ought to go in for plants that do better in shade."

Hercules Potato was only just aware of his hero's musings. As they continued on, he fell to wondering whether the Lady Stella, a Belgian Shepherd and much admired beauty, would also be out for a promenade with her hero, Madame Genevie Bartholomé. This hero and dog, newcomers to Dale-on-Tweedy-Down, first attracted his notice because they were fellow Belgians. However, he soon discovered that the Lady Stella was so much more to him than merely a mutual expatriate. Not that he had yet found any means of relating as much to her.

The enthralling scent of the Lady Stella, much admired beauty, proved to be utterly unmerciful upon the famed detective's intellect. An acute lapse of wits rendered him incapable of intelligent expression whenever she came within his inhaling range. Going completely mute was the best he could manage when fate transpired for them to share the same pavement. She always greeted him politely on these occasions, but her beautiful manners typically increased his symptoms to such an extent that his joints would feel on the point of collapsing beneath him.

As the Lady Stella and her hero Bartholomé lived down the lane running behind Little Marchmain, Hercules Potato did not usually encounter them on their morning rounds. This morning proved to confirm the expected pattern, and he continued on his walk glad and sorry at the same time. As they passed by the tenth house on the left, one Hercules Potato knew to belong to a hero by the name of Jeffries, he discovered new information to occupy his intellect.

The scent of yet another newcomer took hold of his nose, and as he trotted steadily on, glimpses through the slats of the picket fence showed him fresh paw prints in the front garden. The scents and the logic strongly suggested the hero Jeffries had welcomed home a new dog yesterday. He thought to himself that he must return here later in the morning and extend to this new dog a neighborly welcome. After one more pause to accommodate the leg lifting, they circled back and returned to the fifth house, now the one on the right, but still the one with tree swing in the front garden.

As they came into the front hall passage, the grand hero Gwendolyn popped her head out from within the White Room, and asked, "Gavin, dear, I don't suppose you stopped in to see to Mrs. Blevins' cat?"

Hercules Potato shuddered. The grand hero Gavin stopped short. "Why on earth would I have looked in on her cat?"

"Because, dear, I told you, she's gone off on one of those round the world cruises and we're to look after her cat, Misty or Miss Pea, or something to that effect. Oh, well, never mind. I can do it after work. How is the garden this morning, darling?"

"Gwenda, my dear, I only just managed to save the weigela in time. It's been days without water, I suppose?"

"Well it was a bit dry while you were away, dearest, oddly so. I had meant to get the hosepipe out, but I found dust in the White

Room and it slipped my mind entirely. Is your weigela doing very badly?"

"Dry as the Sahara and drooping miserably," he said as he bent down to release the dogs from their leads, "but I have tended to her admirably and I think she will recover. I am going to finish the install on my sprinkler system the moment I come home today. It's just as I said before. It doesn't do to be inconsistent about watering."

Hercules Potato, listening to this discourse, remembered an exchange about a sprinkler system during the dinner hour some weeks ago. He and Pookie Shams had been on duty to assist with health and safety should any food be spilled on the floor, while the grand hero Gavin had outlined his proposal to the family for installing a sprinkler system in the front garden.

As the petite heroes snuck green peas from their plates and slipped them to the two less than grateful dogs below table, the grand hero Gwendolyn had taken a dim view of the proposed project. "I simply don't see the use of our having a sprinkler system, Gavin dearest. To hear you go on about it, one would think we lived in a desert country rather than one famous the world over for its always being rainy."

"Oh, but I shan't have it timed to go off everyday, my dear. I will program it for use only on days when it is dry out. Uniformity and constancy are what a garden needs. It's all well and good to have rainy days end to end, but then what of the sunny days when the grass and the plants must go parched? It's not so bad when I am here to see to their watering personally, but when I am away, it goes unattended."

"I am sorry, dearest, but we do get so busy when you're away. I quite forget—"

"And believe me I understand, but it is precisely why we need this sprinkler system so urgently. I tell you, it's going to be the thing that makes the major difference when I take down Sir Wordsworth Plumms-a-rot at this summer's Best in Beauty."

"Dearest, if you must have this sprinkler system to win your garden contest then by all means install it, but I do wish you wouldn't disparage the aristocracy in front of the children."

Now, after the grand hero Gavin's proclamation that his sprinkler system would become fully operational this very evening, Hercules Potato considered its implications. He must be careful about where he chose to take his outdoor naps in future. The convergence onto a single scene of Pookie Shams, a sprinkler system, and a napping famed detective filled his mind with catastrophic imaginings. However, the sight of the grand hero Gavin taking his cereal bowl from the kitchen table to the sink brought the dog back to awareness of more present troubles.

More days than not, it seemed, the morning routine contained two decidedly undesirable events. The first of these typically unfolded shortly after their walk. The grand hero Gavin would place his cereal bowl in the kitchen sink, take a last sip from his beaker of coffee, kiss the grand hero Gwendolyn, and kiss the petite heroes Lewis and Montcy. He would then come, as he came now, to pat the heads of Hercules Potato and Pookie Shams. "You fellows be good today. Don't go letting any burglars in if you can help it."

He turned and went out of the kitchen and down the front hall passage. The two dogs followed after him. He took his well-worn Burberry from the passage closet, grabbed his briefcase, and then disappeared out of the front door. As both dogs sniffed after him, they heard the grand hero Gwendolyn say, "Montcy, dear, do stop dawdling and go and get your rucksack. Mummy has an early meeting today."

As the petite hero Montcy clambered upstairs, the two dogs darted to the dining room and lept onto the window seat and pressed their faces against the windowpanes. They watched the grand hero Gavin walking down the reclaimed stone pathway. Before he opened the front gate, he stooped down to reinspect the weigela. Evidently, he was pleased with the patient's progress, for he nodded his head approvingly and stood back up and went whistling out the front gate. As he disappeared up the crest of the lane towards the High Street, Hercules Potato thought to himself, always it happens this way, but our hero, always he returns.

In the next minute, better news arrived when they heard the grand hero Gwendolyn say, "Lewis, darling, put some food in the dogs' bowls, and look sharp about it. Daddy's already off to the station, and we must be getting along as well."

Hercules Potato and Pookie Shams raced back down the front hall passage towards the kitchen to the delightful tune of their own bowls being filled with food. The two dogs made quick work of their allotted portions. Pookie Shams then began to helpfully sniff along the periphery of the kitchen floor in order to clean any remaining scraps of fallen food. Hercules Potato followed along in his wake to inspect his housemate's thoroughness.

"Slipshod, *comme d'habitude*," he muttered to himself.

The petite hero Lewis, observing this scene, pointed it out to the grand hero Gwendolyn, saying, "Mum, look how much Hercules Potato loves Pookie Shams, he follows him everywhere."

"Yes, dearest," said the grand hero Gwendolyn absently, as she attempted to flatten a cowlick on the boy's head. "Of course he does." She leaned down and patted Hercules Potato's head. "Go get her, fellow. Go get Montcy."

Hercules Potato understood what was expected of him. He shot out straight away to call the tardy petite hero to order. Pookie Shams followed after him up the stairs, having got hold of some notion of things going on he might wish to be included in. They burst into the little bedroom to find the petite hero Montcy locked in a determined struggle to attach a large rucksack onto her small shoulders.

"Hello, fellows," she greeted them.

Pookie Shams illegally sprang onto the bed to lick her face. Hercules Potato, who believed in the rule of law, admonished the miscreant with a sharp, "Jappe, jappe, jappe."

The petite hero Montcy frowned at him, then she scolded, "No, Hercules Potato. You mustn't bullyrag poor little Pookie Shams. He can lick my face if he wants to."

She hugged Pookie Shams and shook her head disapprovingly at Hercules Potato as she left the room. Pookie Shams jumped down from the bed and kept close at her heels. Hercules Potato sniffed the feet of a pretty, curly haired doll sitting nearby in her little chair. He said to her, "Ah, *mam'zelle, c'est vrai,* the order and the way of things, they are not understood by the petite heroes, *n'est-ce pas?*"

He trotted out of the bedroom and went down stairs just in time to see the front door close and to hear the lock click-to. This was the second of the aforementioned undesirable events so often occurring of a morning. He went once again to the window seat to watch his heroes motor out of the drive. He faced yet another endless day filled with nothing other than the unstimulating company of Pookie Shams.

As the Thistlewait motorcar departed, Hercules Potato noticed another figure observing the sad scene. This one sat erect and alert at the edge of the front garden across the lane. Hercules Potato knew from long experience with this dog, that he was waiting for a precise moment, a moment chosen according to a carefully thought out strategy, in which to make his move. It was his friend, the Colonel, celebrated leader of the Dogs of Dawn.

For years, this indefatigable Airedale enjoyed substantial reputation as the fearless leader of a regiment of rescue dogs. Now in his retirement, he still epitomised duty as dogs properly understand the word to mean. In his day, after earthquakes, fires, and floods the world over, when the Colonel and his 42nd Rescue Rainbow Regiment of Paw arrived on the scene of disaster, they rescued heroes from death, alleviated crushing sorrow, and restored much hope in the midst of upheaval and grief.

Their official name not withstanding, these fearless rescuers came to be known as the Dogs of Dawn. Many stories circulated, particularly ones featuring the Colonel, of dogs who entered smoke-filled houses to pull out trapped petite heroes, of many dives from helicopters into frigid lakes to save drowning heroes, and of daring climbs to great heights to bring ropes to climbing heroes who had got themselves trapped on mountain ledges.

Seizing his moment this morning, the Colonel crossed the lane, scrabbled through a gap in Portuguese laurel, gained the front garden of the fifth house on the left, passed by the tree swing, and went around to the rear of the house, where he knew he would find his entry point. It did not escape Hercules Potato's notice that the Colonel wore his old uniform today, a distinguished red rescue vest, which bore the circular crest, "42nd Rainbow Rescue Regiment of Paw, Dogs of Dawn," with its emblematic, black paw stamped in its center.

"So," said Hercules Potato, famed detective, "this is not the call social. The Colonel, he comes on business."

CHAPTER II

THE CLIENT MOST DREADFUL

*H*ercules Potato trotted off to the kitchen, just in time to see the Colonel emerging through the dog's door.

"Ah, good morning to you, Potato," he said briskly, coming up to sniff his friend.

"*Bonjour, le* Colonel. It goes well with you today?"

19

"The world is going to the cats as usual, Potato, but we are managing to keep the castle for now."

"*Très bien*, Colonel, and can I offer you a sip of the water from my bowl?"

"You're a good egg to offer, Potato, but I'm not here to share pleasantries. I come on serious business. There's a case I want you on sharpish, and I am going to get right down to brass tacks."

"*Ah, bien*, so I deduced, Colonel. If you will please to seat your-self, I am at leisure to hear what is your case." The Colonel nodded satisfactorily and made himself comfortable on a plush spot of carpet near where Hercules Potato sat down on his kitchen cushion.

"I suppose," began the Colonel, "you are aware of this new dog staying with the hero Jefferies?"

Hercules Potato said, "*Oui*, I smelled as much this morning, *merveilleux, n'est-ce pas*? I have not been round yet to extend my welcome to this new dog, but I shall in due course."

"It is not as simple as you put it, Potato," cut in the Colonel, shaking his head emphatically. "I gather from your reaction you consider the hero Jefferies to be the putative hero of this dog?"

"Naturally," responded Hercules Potato rather taken aback. "And I gather from your reaction you do not? Why do you imply of the hero Jefferies, he is not the rightful hero of this new dog?" He eyed the Colonel warily as he probed him. "You do not attach a scandal of any kind to the presence of this dog on our lane most fair?"

"Since you put it that way, old boy, in fact I do attach scandal to it and quite the worst kind of scandal possible."

Hercules Potato waited for him to continue, but the Colonel seemed to think Hercules Potato now knew quite enough to state the case himself. A moment or two of silence transpired before the Colonel, the ever fearless, oft impatient, celebrated leader of the Dogs of Dawn, saw he needed to push things along more firmly. "Don't be so ruddy blind, confound you. Are you or are you not the famed detective? I thought I could rely on you, Potato, out of everyone, to be able to see this new dog is most certainly a lost dog."

"A lost dog?" queried Hercules Potato.

"Yes, to drive the thing home, a lost dog. I have spoken with her, and I have established as fact that her presence here correlates to a hero who is somewhere else, at this very moment, in severe emotional distress from missing her."

"If this is the case, I am sure the hero Jeffries, he will do what is just and necessary for the lost dog. He will find her hero for her and return her to whomever it is."

"Do you actually think so, Potato? It is only the next day since the hero Jeffries found her, and already I see he is in small way attached to her. She has no collar, no means of identification. No one in Dale-on-Tweedy-Down recognises her. There being no easy or obvious means of tracing her hero, I don't anticipate the hero Jeffries will stir himself to make many more enquiries on her behalf."

Hercules Potato continued to delicately test the waters of doubt. "Perhaps it is best, *n'est-ce pas?*"

"Best," barked the Colonel jumping up. "Best? How is it best? I should very much like to hear you tell me, Potato, how it is best." The Colonel, however, did not wait to be told. He delivered the telling himself. "I tell you, it is not best. It is outrageous, and we must do everything possible to press for restoration."

"H'm, *moi*, I think it is the bad idea."

"Do you? Think it a bad idea? You must tell me why you say it is a bad idea. I can tell you— "

"Ah, if you please, Colonel," interjected Hercules Potato holding up a paw. "Give me the word in edgeways *s'il tu plaît*, and I shall explain to you my thoughts."

The Colonel glared at him, but he sat down again and waited to hear more.

"*Bien*, my thoughts, they are these. If, as you suggest, the first hero exists, than it is possible to imagine this figure to have accepted the loss of this dog and to go on with the life. Perhaps, this is even one of those mystifying antiheroes who send their dogs away from them."

"Don't be preposterous, Potato."

"If I may please to finish. In any case, she is now settled to the joy and fondness of the hero Jeffries. It will be a sorrow to him, a hero whom we know and trust, if we alert the former hero, whom we do not know and trust, to her new location. *Donc*, it is why I say it may be best to let everything advance according to this fate. I propose to you not to muddle in the past, Colonel."

The exasperated Airedale could take no more of this. "Don't be such a busted Belgian, Potato. I expect you to show a little vision here."

Hercules Potato bristled, but the Colonel barreled on, giving him no time to demand satisfaction of his besmirched, national honour. "You are talking like a perfect cat, Potato. I can't believe my ears. Now look here, I am not talking about the past. I am talking about what happened yesterday. Yes-ter-day."

He paused to let this sink in while Hercules Potato drummed his paw meditatively on the floor.

"Today's suffering is a present distress. To hear you put it, anyone might think this lost dog showed up a decade ago. Not so. We have a duty to fulfill in this matter. Good. She is a lost dog. The foundation of our society depends upon her being restored to her true hero, the hero who lost her. I understand the hero Jefferies might be disappointed to lose her, but it is a natural kind of disappointment he will at once accept the moment he sees the true hero and the beloved dog reunited."

Smoothing his beard and moustache, the famed detective mused over the Colonel's reading of crisis in the situation. "*Bien*, Colonel, and what if I come to agree with you? If I too say, '*Oui*, the hero of this lost dog must be found. The two must be restored to each other.' Who is going to, as it were, bell the cat?"

The Colonel goggled at him. "I should have thought it was obvious from the beginning, old boy. This lost dog is to be your client. The true hero must be traced and brought here to reclaim her. That is the case. Who is the lost dog's true hero and where is this true hero to be found? It is you, the famed detective, who must solve these questions. You must use that thing, er, what is it you are always going on about?"

"The logic and the scents."

"Yes, that's the one, use the good old logic and scents to help find the hero and find a way to bring the hero back here to be reunited with your client, our lost dog."

"Colonel, you speak of my being the famed detective as though you think I am also the famed magician. I do not merely wave my nose in the air, trace a few smells and say, '*Et voila*, here is the true hero.'"

The Colonel, celebrated leader of the Dogs of Dawn, was not one to let overly artistic and dramatic objections carry sway with him. "I have no supernatural expectations of you, rest assured, so enough with the argle-bargle. All I want you to do is to come to the hero Jefferies' home and speak with this lost dog. I am sure you will find her case a compelling one. Ask her the questions which naturally occur to you to ask, and you can suss out from her answers any clues you need to get started on the case."

Hercules Potato considered this suggestion. Before the Colonel's visit, he had only a long, tedious day stretched out before him, with no company other than the doltish Pookie Shams. He turned his head towards the window and saw that hapless dog trotting along the roof of the back garden shed. He watched as Pookie Shams slipped, then fell with a whimper off of the roof and onto a pile of rubbish bags queued up to await removal day. Hercules Potato turned back to the Colonel and said, "*Bien*, I will come later for a chat with this lost dog."

"Excellent, that's the stuff we want, old chap."

"Ah, just the chat, it is all I say right now," insisted Hercules

Potato. "I will hear what this lost dog has to say, but I make no promises that I will hear enough to be convinced of accepting the case."

"Of course, of course," assuaged the Colonel. "Nothing needs to be decided yet. I will go over to the hero Jeffries now and inform your client to be ready to receive a visit from you. Come along shortly, and after you hear what she has to say, then we can discuss what needs must be our battle plan."

Hercules Potato called out after the celebrated leader of the Dogs of Dawn, now advancing through the dog's door, "It might be," he cried, "after I speak with this lost dog, the only thing 'needs must' is for me to needs must take the afternoon nap."

The sight of the flapping dog's door told him his last words had been completely thrown away.

AFTER HIS DEBATE with the Colonel, Hercules Potato ambled over to his water bowl and took a few sips, being careful to save some of it for later. He returned to his kitchen cushion to take a small rest before he set off to interview the prospective client. While he dosed off, Pookie Shams pottered into the kitchen and drained first his own water bowl, and then what water remained in Hercules Potato's bowl.

At length, he retired upstairs to enjoy a nap on one of the heroes' tempting beds. When Hercules Potato awoke shortly thereafter, he found to his chagrin he could not take his post-nap sip of water. Not for the first time, he thought how much his home life would improve if Pookie Shams exhibited the same perpetual thirst for knowledge as he did for drinking water not his own.

With the expectation of water being available at the hero Jeffries' establishment, Hercules Potato slipped through the dog's door, rounded the house, and scraped his way through an out of the way corner in the Portuguese laurel. This brought him onto the pavement lining the lane, and he decided to cross it and to go to the home of the Colonel first, in order to check if he was waiting for him there.

The Colonel, he considered, may have decided to wait for Hercules Potato at his own home rather than at the hero Jeffries. Hercules Potato felt it would be awkward to arrive alone at the strange dog's threshold, without the benefit of company with one who had already been introduced to her.

He first ran a paw through his beard and moustache to ensure no leaves or debris clung to his otherwise immaculate visage. He glanced down at his spat like ankles and felt at once assured of his elegant appearance. As he stopped to make sure the lane was free of the threat of motorcars, a divine scent began to curve winsomely through his nostrils.

In the next moment, the purveyor of this cherished scent appeared at the crest of the hill up the lane. There she stood, a dazzling vision of jet-black fur, sleek and gleaming in the morning sunlight. As she floated towards him, he beheld her deep, brown eyes sparkling like two enchanted spirits. The joints in his tiny legs began to go blooey.

At seeing Hercules Potato, placed as he was with two front paws on the lane and two back paws on the pavement, the Lady Stella must have wondered what his purpose could have possibly been, but, as always, she was polite, and she only said, "*Bonjour, monsieur* Potato."

Her voice, redolent as it was of silks and satins, did nothing to help Hercules Potato find his own paltry voice. For his part, he continued standing there just as he was, wholly unable to think of anything to contribute verbally to the record of the proceeding. After a long pause, the Lady Stella said, "How odd you do look, *Monsieur*. Is it that you mean to cross the lane, or is it that you mean to return onto the pavement?"

Hercules Potato could not remember. It seemed to him he

might have, at one time, formed an intention to cross the lane, but just now he could not be sure.

"Why, *Monsieur*, you are quivering like so many leaves in a reedy tree. You are unwell? You have maybe *la maladie?*"

Hercules Potato continued to find no words with which he could make her an immediate answer. In a ploy to purchase a bit more time, he extended to her a gracious and slow bow. "The Lady Stella," he managed to squeak as his nose brushed the ground. "It is a pleasure to see you on so fine a day as this one."

He now found inner strength enough to meet her eyes, which sparkled down at him from high above. A Belgian Shepherd is, of course, in an altogether separate percentile from that of a Belgian Griffon, and indeed, heroes typically referred to the Lady Stella as a large dog.

She returned this small dog's greeting benevolently, saying, "I hope always to hear a phrase friendly from you, *monsieur* Potato, but you should return home to your cushion if you are unwell."

"*Non, non*, the Lady Stella. I assure you, Hercules Potato, he is the picture of health. I felt only the touch of a slight breeze as you came by, *c'est tout.*" He stared longingly up at her. There was so much he wanted to say to her, but the words he needed were, as they always were in her presence, pure pandemonium in his head. Here, on this pavement of perfect opportunity, he once again squandered what could have added so much to his happiness, managing only to say, "The Lady Stella, did you know?"

The Lady Stella waited patiently to hear more, but no more came. Hercules Potato began to be that reedy tree of quivering leaves all over again.

"*Quoi,*" she pressed him, "Do I know what, *monsieur* Potato?"

Hercules Potato shook himself, then he sputtered out, "We are both Belgian."

The Lady Stella laughed, a delightful, truthful, merry laugh, and then she said, "You are a droll little dog, monsieur Potato I am sure that I do not know any dog as delightfully intriguing as you are. Of course, *c'est vrai,* it is as you say, we are *tous les deux* Belgians."

Hercules Potato blushed beneath his beard and moustache. Before he could have been expected to say more, however, a far-a-way voice intruded into their *tête-a-tête.* "Lady Stella, *vient ici,* Lady Stella. Come home, *ma fille.*"

"Ah," said the Lady Stella. "That is, as they say, the call from headquarters. My hero, she does so rely upon me for the support emotional. I like never to leave her alone for very long. She wants that I am with her when she does her breathing exercises. *Au revoir, monsieur* Potato."

The Lady Stella turned her magnificent figure homeward and was gone. A few minutes later, in a barely audible whisper, Hercules Potato managed to say, "*Au revoir,* the Lady Stella."

Eventually, he did remember his intention to find the Colonel at his home, but going there, discovered him absent. The spell the Lady Stella had cast over him remained all the while, and even as he entered into the quiet front garden of the hero Jeffries, he did so as one who must enter the staid confines of reality after wandering back from some faraway, enchanted realm.

Even as he began to recover his bearings and to sniff about the front garden, he thought of the hero bard Shakespeare's donkey Bottom and the Queen Titania, tucked away companionably in their midsummer's dream. He wondered, if in his own world governed as it was by the scents and the logic, such a love spell as came over them could come over the Lady Stella and himself? *Non*, he thought. The things spiritual, they are all nonsense. The scents and the logic hold no truck with love spells.

The general atmosphere of the hero Jeffries front garden confirmed what Hercules Potato had sensed about it from the lane earlier in the morning. He smelled all of the telltale scents of a newly arrived canine. These combined with the scents of the *flora* and *fauna* typical to a front garden, and contributed a wonderful depth of smell.

Hercules Potato mounted the front porch steps and surveyed the scene. He noted the places where soft soil glowed under the blessings of freshly pressed paw prints, and thought that here was a front garden that had at last come into its fullest purpose for existing. For what can be the use of so charming a garden if it does not play host to a dog? He felt a slight pang. He was here on a purpose, which, if the Colonel had his way, would wrest from this lawn the best happiness yet known to it.

The Colonel, still in his uniform, came around from the back of the house and caught site of Hercules Potato, perched on the front porch and gazing starry-eyed at the front garden. "Great Scott, Potato, you're late. Stop standing there like you're waiting for Father Christmas and get round here to the back of the house."

That stuck the final pinprick into his dream bubble, and Hercules Potato shook himself out vigorously. He followed the Colonel around to the back of the house and they made their way to a screened-in porch. Its door was propped open by a string tied through the handle and attached to a stake in the ground. The two dogs mounted three small steps and entered into the pleasant interior. A soft carpet spread out over the cement floor, and a bowl of water glittered in the far corner.

Hercules Potato noticed it directly, and then saw out of the corner of his eye a dingy chew toy lying near the water bowl. Next, he looked to a wicker settee, covered in plush cushions and draped by a rug. A tremendous presence lounged upon it. Hercules Potato lifted his eyes upwards and beheld an awe-inspiring animal.

Lengths of flowing ivory tresses sheathed her majestic body, her graceful and regal head curved nobly down into a most perfect muzzle. Hercules Potato, Belgian Griffon and famed detective, knew upon sight she was a Borzoi, one who hailed from a fierce and swift breed of hunters, of whom legend whispered tales of noble and ferocious deeds. If one sought beauty in a dog, one would find it in a Borzoi. A reverent respecter of beauty, he nonetheless felt she did not quite match the standard set by the Lady Stella. He anticipated, however, that a conversation with her would be one of profound, intellectual interest.

The Colonel reverently bowed before the resplendent animal as he said, "Your Imperial Highness, allow me to present to you Mr. Hercules Potato."

The magnificent Borzoi nodded her assent, and the Colonel then turned to his friend and said, "Hercules Potato, it is my honour to introduce you to her Imperial Highness, the Princess Anastazia."

Hercules Potato stared back at the Colonel in disbelief as he said, "*Vraiment*, this is indeed amazing, Colonel, to have left out this detail most extraordinary when you came to speak to me earlier."

The Colonel, unapologetic, said, "Need to know basis and what, what, Potato."

The famed detective then became aware of a long, white muzzle leaning down and sniffing at his collar. He turned to see the Borzoi's imperious face gazing into his own. Her expression plainly gave away that she questioned the worth of this trespass upon her time. His hope for intellectual stimulation melted away. Haughty dogs rarely ever prove brilliant conversationalists, and this dog clearly had a haughty bent to her.

Hercules Potato greeted her, *"Je suis enchanté de vous rencontrer, Princess Anastazia,"* only slightly bowing his head to her. "It is a pleasure to make your acquaintance." He thought to himself that this would be the hospitable moment for her to offer to him to take a small sip of water from her bowl.

The Princess Anastazia did not nod in return, nor did she offer her guest a sip of water from her bowl. She raised her lofty muzzle on high and peered down at him through narrowed, impervious eyes. "Potato?" She asked in a voice steeped in ancestral pride, "Potato is it?"

Hercules Potato obfuscated her slighting question and continued to attempt to make pleasantries. *"Mam'zelle,* there is a not-so-very-nice cat who lives two doors up from this house, but I hope she has not been by here to give you any trouble."

"We have seen no cats since coming here. We object to cats, naturally, and we never speak to them. We make no exceptions to our policy, not even in this strange place."

Hercules Potato said, *"Moi,* I cannot entirely agree with you on this point. The cat I mention, it is true, she demonstrates the behavior objectionable, and she is not agreeable to take into conversation. Nonetheless, while cats are the creatures most puzzling to me, I cannot agree that it is never worthwhile to engage them."

The Princess Anastazia did not pursue the topic further. She turned to the Colonel and said, "Are we to understand this is the detective you spoke of?"

"Yes, your highness, this is the famed detective Hercules Potato," answered the Colonel. Seeing doubt in her looks, he hastened to add, "Eh, please allow me to assure you he is a stalwart old thing. You can trust in his abilities implicitly."

Hercules Potato cast a sideways glance at the Colonel, annoyed that the celebrated leader of the Dogs of Dawn could be so hopelessly overcome by a dubious claim to nobility.

The princess directed her gaze again at the small Belgian Griffon before her, now with a more studious penetration. "Is that true?" she asked at last. "We had expected something more along the lines of a German Shepard to aid our cause, but you are exceedingly small. Are you the famed detective, and do you present your services here at the hour of our greatest need?"

Hercules Potato rankled beneath her contempt, but he answered, "It is true, Princess Anastazia, I am the famed detective, Hercules Potato, but I cannot yet make you the promise to place myself in your service. First, I must hear what you have to say about your journey to my beautiful village. What, *par example*, is the name of the village or town to which you belong?"

A shadow crossed the royal face, and she said, "We live in a palace. There is a village somewhere nearby, but we cannot remember what it is called." She once again directed her gaze at the Colonel. Her look strongly suggested he should clarify his meaning in bringing such an upstart as this Hercules Potato into her presence.

The Colonel cleared his throat, and then he urged her, "Now then, your highness, give old Potato here a chance to collect himself. It is not everyday he engages with royalty after all, and he is a little overcome by your bearing. That is all."

Hercules Potato snorted.

The Colonel, sensing an impending rebellion, attempted further conciliation. "Please, I beg you, if your highness will just tell Hercules Potato your story, of how you come to be here, in the house of the hero Jeffries, in our village of Dale-on-Tweedy-Down. I think then we will all begin to see things proceed to a better point. We also must decide how to best proceed with the problem of your not having the proper identification. No tags, no collar, it could be quite difficult, as you know."

The princess sniffed, and said, "We are of a long line of benevolent potentates, and we do not often allow ourselves to be taken up in this way by the weariness of peasants, but very well. You shall hear all about our misfortune in due course. We do not have our identification, it is true, but we do have our royal chew toy. It will serve as sufficient proof of who we are." She archly directed their gaze with her muzzle over to the chew toy Hercules Potato had first noticed when he came in.

He remained manifestly unimpressed by it. Faded strings of what must have once been brightly coloured threads, trailed down from a body of braided but extremely dirty ropes. He did not consider it to have the slightest aspect of royalty about it. Indeed, it could have slid in among Pookie Shams' own ignoble collection of chew toys without causing the least comment.

"You came all that way with your chew toy, Your Highness?" asked the Colonel. "It is indeed most impressive."

"Yes, well," she said, "We are never parted from our royal chew toy." She sniffed again, and then said, "Our story is a simple one." Here, she cast another look at Hercules Potato, as if to ask, "Does he understand this word, 'simple?'"

Hercules Potato rolled his eyes. He lay down on the carpet and made himself tolerably comfortable. From time to time, his eyes drifted over to the water bowl in the corner.

"We were strolling outside the grounds of the palace yesterday morning. The royal bath had just been completed, and we wanted the fresh air to dry our royal locks." Her tone reflected deep regret as she explained, "It was the royal bath, you see, that began all of our subsequent troubles. Our hero ordered our royal collar be removed for our bath, as it is want to stain our white coat purple if it becomes wet. That is how we came to appear in public without our royal signet. Alas, as the sunlight graced us, the scent of chocolate flew in on a delightful breeze, and we had no thought other than to chase after it. We had our royal chew toy in our mouth, and we pursued the scent across the great lawn, downward upon the drive, and through the palace gates into the lowly streets. We—"

"Ah, *excusez-moi*," interrupted the famed detective, "Princess, please to answer just one question."

She peered down at him in the manner of one greatly put upon. "If you must ask, we will entertain your question."

Hercules Potato suppressed a sarcastic chortle and said, "These gates of which you speak, *normalement*, they remain open?"

Her brow lifted slightly, as she considered the question. "No, it is not normal, not in the slightest. The gates are always closed, unless they open for our hero to come and go in his motorcar."

"Yet not yesterday," he asked, "Why were they open yesterday?"

The Princess Anastazia again cast him a glance of much exhausted patience.

The Colonel cleared his throat and said, "I say, old chap, we can come back to the point if need be, but do let her Royal Highness get on with it."

Hercules Potato resigned in agreement and signaled to the princess to continue.

She gave a long sniff then went on. "As we said, we followed the scent into the lowly street below the palace gates. It became a longer chase than we first anticipated, but we did eventually sniff the chocolate to earth when we came through a path in the wood. We found many stacks of boxes we could smell to be filled with chocolates. They were all in piles outside of a building, and there were many worker heroes busily transferring these boxes filled with chocolates into motorised conveyances. We went up to these worker heroes, to demand our right of royal portion, but they were impudent and denied us our share. They tried to cover their treason by whispering nonsense about chocolate being bad for dogs, saying it can kill dogs even. Marauders, all of them."

"It is most true, Princess Anastazia," said Hercules Potato. "*Moi,*

33

I have heard my own heroes refuse to give me chocolate upon the same reasoning. Chocolate, they say, it is the killer of the dogs."

"Lies of usurpers."

"Now, now, Your Highness," assuaged the Colonel, "you were making excellent progress with your tale. Come, come, and tell us what happened next."

The Princess Anastazia shook out her coat in effort to restore her calm, and then she resumed where she left off. "We began to think of returning to the palace, and we started away from the scent of chocolate, but we soon realised we went out by the wrong road. Just as we made ready to reverse our course, the scent of fish, delicious fish, assailed our nose anew and urged us to follow after it. How could we resist it? The scent took us across a field and to a river. We could see it full of fish, jumping in and out of the water as they rushed past. We dove in and splashed about, catching much and feasting marvellously. When we were fully satisfied, we began to think again of home and the royal palace, but as we began to sniff about for our direction, the scent of chickens took us in its power."

Hercules Potato again interrupted her narrative. "But surely, Princess Anastazia, you were not hungry? You say you had just filled yourself full of the fish. Why did you then go chasing greedily after some chickens?"

"Outrageous impudence," cried the Princess Anastazia. "How dare you accuse us of such baseness?"

"Steady on, Potato," said the Colonel wearily. "If you would just let her get on with her recollections. It is after all terribly important for us to hear these details. Good." Turning back to the princess, he said, "Your Highness, you said the scent began as one of chocolate, then proceeded to one of fish? Good. Now you bring in chickens. Is this a correct assessment of the information so far?"

"Yes, you show yourself admirably informed," said the Princess Anastazia, "but why cannot you take this intermeddling little dog away?" She fixed upon Hercules Potato an expression flooded with imperial wroth, and Hercules Potato almost thought she might be royalty of some sort after all.

"I beg your highness will extend him your gracious and beneficent patience for a little longer," pled the Colonel. "Hercules Potato is a most excellent dog, and we will not be able to see you restored to your palace and your true hero without him."

Hercules Potato, despite thinking this princess was the epitome of anything and everything that ever made itself perfectly ridiculous, felt nonetheless gratified by the Colonel's commendation of him. So, he gave way and said, "Please, Princess Anastazia, please to continue. I promise you, I make no more the interruptions."

She sniffed and raised her haughty muzzle high as she stood upon all fours to stretch out her limbs. "The rest is a blur you understand. Conditions were intolerable. The chickens. Oh! They were wild, vicious creatures. They were too terrible to even think of eating. We barely escaped with our life."

Hercules Potato held his tongue, but noting again her giant, statuesque figure, he wondered at how things had come to pass on the earth that a puny little chicken could best a mighty Borzoi.

The princess lowered her muzzle and settled down on the settee again. "After we escaped the chickens, we stumbled into a new place, our frazzled nerves cannot recall its form, but we do remember the scent of dead roses. That is all we can remember there. We were in dire distress, and we wandered on and on, until we reached a glen with a little brook running through it. It is where this hero Jeffries, as you call him, found us."

"Yes, yes, quite right," said the excited Colonel. "He found you down the lane in the glen, alongside the brook, and brought you here. Now, I know he rather admires you, and it is a comfortable enough home for a dog here, but it is not your palace, is it? He is not your true hero, is he?"

"No, it is just as you say. We are not in our kingdom, and we wish to be restored to it."

"How now, Potato?" asked the Colonel. "What say you? Can you, the famed detective, retrace these scents and regain this lost princess's kingdom for her?"

"Yes, can you restore us to our kingdom?" asked the Princess Anastazia, her voice still brimming with skepticism. "If you do, you shall have the royal remembrance from us."

Hercules Potato wondered with lifted brow just what a Belgian Griffon, however famed a detective, would be expected to do with a "royal remembrance"? It sounded to him like a thing about as useful and worthwhile as a doorknob. He rose to sit back on his haunches. "*Oui, c'est possible*, I could be of assistance to you, Princess Anastazia."

The Colonel beamed at him with a pleased expression, and Hercules Potato said, "I think the best plan, it is for the Colonel and myself to accompany you back along the paths you traveled to reach Dale-on-Tweedy-Down. We can assist you in detecting the scents remembered by you, and the sights familiar will no doubt come back to you and help guide you safely home once we leave you to return home ourselves. You with us, us with you, that should speed the whole business along with the desirable quickness."

The face of the Princess Anastazia filled with chagrin. Raising herself up once more, she made her final pronouncement. "That is not our will and pleasure. We shall remain here."

Hercules Potato turned to the Colonel and said, "Colonel, if we might now have a word together in private?"

At which point, no longer feeling the need to stand upon ceremony, he went over to the princess' water bowl and took from it a long and enjoyable drink.

⁓

CHAPTER III

A BRIGHT AND SPORTY ASSISTANT

"I take it," said the Colonel as they filed down the porch steps, "you see what needs be done as clearly as I do?"

Hercules Potato stopped to shake out the water droplets from his beard and moustache, then he smoothed out his fur with his paw before he said, "*Non*, Colonel. I do not have such clarity as

37

you seem to possess. This lost dog, as you so nicely called her this morning, she is the client most dreadful. Why did you not tell to me before that she styles herself a princess?"

"Shhh," said the Colonel anxiously as they trotted towards a patch of sunshine in center of the hero Jefferies back garden, "In hugger mugger, if you please, Potato. I chose not to broadcast to the entire village that royalty is come to it. We'll have every last dog in the village coming round to get a look at her if they so much as get a whiff of her nobility."

"Humph, that is as may be, Colonel, but it changes nothing. Why should I agree to take on her case when she is so horribly superior to life itself?"

They reached the sunshine patch and the celebrated leader of the Dogs of Dawn turned to face the famed detective. Raising himself to his fullest height, he said, "Because it is not for her alone you will act. You will act on behalf of the natural order of the universe; you will act to uphold the natural law itself. A law not written by heroes or made by dogs, but which exists outside of all of us, and makes us to understand that a dog must be with its hero. It is by this natural law that we know our heroes cannot live in any joy while they are separated from their dogs. It is by this natural law that we know only death is permitted to sever dog from hero for the rest of time. One ill-chosen walk to investigate the scent of chocolate must not be allowed to stand as an event powerful enough to separate dog and hero forever while both yet live. This is why you must act, Potato. It is not for the princess alone. It is for the sake of every dog who owes a duty to a hero. It is for the sake of every hero who loves and is loved by a dog."

Hercules Potato felt a rush of canine pride despite himself. He considered the hero philosopher Socrates, speaking some two thousand years ago, could not have stated a better case for the nature of reality. The Colonel, for all his bullyragging, knew how to motivate a reluctant dog to run willingly to the path of undesired duty.

The famed detective answered, *"Oui d'accord.* I accept the case."

"At last, something worth hearing from you, Potato. Good. We must turn our thoughts to strategy and to executing specifics."

"I fear it will not be easy," said Hercules Potato. "As no one here recognises the princess, I think she must have come from far away. Worse, there is this: if she will not come with us, then even if we find her true hero, how do we tell our good news that we know where the lost princess can to be found? If she came with us, it would be a matter most simple to present her at the proper doorstep, *et voila.* It would be clear to her hero what is going on. *Mais non,* she is stubborn and she will not do this much for herself. What will we do when we arrive at this so called palace?"

"Nonsense, Potato, all you lack is a clear plan. Once you have one, you can trust the rest to the magic of heroes."

Hercules Potato growled and said, "Colonel, there you go again with the thoughts magical, but Hercules Potato, he does not work by the magic, *non.* He works by the scents and the logic, by the things *parfaitement rationelle, c'est tout.*"

"Oh do keep your fur on, Potato. I only meant that heroes have such useful, if somewhat mystifying talents, despite their severe limitations, of course. Whoever this hero is will find you on the palace doorstep and believe you to be a lost dog yourself. My knowledge of hero behavior is sufficient to foresee what will occur next."

"Is that so?"

"Naturally, it is so. Look here, upon seeing an unfamiliar dog upon the palace threshold, the hero will stoop down to read your tag. He will then call out a few numbers, punch some buttons on one of those bizarre contraptions they are forever talking into, and then you will see the good that comes of it. There will be a little bit of puzzling, one-way conversation, and soon after the monologue ends, your heroes will materialise like magic—no, no," the Colonel held up a front paw up to rebut the anticipated objection. "I know, the word offends you, so you must let me revise it. Your heroes will arrive on the scene in due course as the result of what is no doubt a deeply embedded, logical, and rational aspect within the character of a bizarre contraption. That is all I meant by my slight and insignificant reference to magic."

Hercules Potato felt far from mollified, but the Colonel continued on. "What it comes down to is I have every hope in the world for this meeting of your heroes with the palace hero to result in the mention of the palace hero's lost dog. Your heroes will then say they know precisely where to find the palace hero's lost dog. Then happy day, you will have victoriously solved your case and righted the gone astray course of one hero and one dog."

"The hope is it? Hope is not something the scents and the logic know anything about either."

"No? Well, let me tell you something, Potato. Hope is certainly something a rescue dog knows a lot about. There are certain things of a spiritual nature that are just as real as any scent in a blade of grass or any logic in a tossed ball."

Hercules Potato snorted, but the Colonel took no notice of him and continued on with his outline of strategy. "If you will but allow me to proceed, I have a plan that is simplicity itself. We have four scents, and it is clear enough to me if following the four scents brought the Princess Anastazia to Dale-on-Tweedy-Down, then following the four scents in reverse order will get you back to where she started from — the palace and the true hero. As I said, simple."

"Eh, Colonel," said in Hercules Potato, "you speak of following these four scents all the way back to the palace as though it is going to be as easy as following the scent of a roast from the bedroom to the kitchen. *Mais non*, there could be many difficulties."

As if to help him emphasize his point, a dandelion puff drifted onto his nose and he sneezed. He shook himself, cleared his nose as politely as possible, then picked back up where he left off. "The scents might have washed away in the water that falls from the sky, or become degraded by the moles that crawl up from the ground and mix up the dirt. It is an extraordinary feat which you propose for us."

"Come tardy off, Potato. You exaggerate too much. 'Things in heaven and things under the earth,' blather, blather, blather. It's all a lot of bally whatnot. I know you. You can do this. Good. The plan is simple. As I said, four scents, four points, and there you have it, a Four Point Plan for a successful mission."

The Colonel, who had been sitting upright during this back and forth, now took his ease and lay down in the warm grass of the sunshine patch while he continued to present the details of his plan. "As to your specific objections, there was no rain last night to wash away any of the scents. You are the one who can always smell rain coming while it's still an entire day away, you tell me, is it likely to rain today or even tomorrow?"

Hercules Potato put his nose in the air and sniffed meditatively at the intelligence drifting in the air about him. "*Non,*" he answered reluctantly, "there is no indication of any rain today or tomorrow."

"Good. Now as to your concerns about moles, I hope I do not yet live in a world where a mole is able to stop a dog from smelling something." He reached forward and made a mark in the soil as he said, "Beginning with this first scent, this scent of dead roses. I propose you start nosing around for it in the glen, where the path runs along the brook. That is, after all, where the hero Jeffries found the Princess Anastazia wandering about. When you find it, follow after it until you come to the next scent." He made a second mark in the soil and said, "That is going to be the chickens, and—"

"And what if it is not so clear, eh?" demanded Hercules Potato, lying down beside him. He touched the first mark in the soil with his paw as he said, "First of all, how do we find this first scent so obscure? Do you think we will just go trip, trip, tripping through the tulips *et volia*, there will be the dead roses? What if the scent of the dead roses does not say, 'here now, Hercules Potato, is the scent of the chickens. You must go following it because our scent is now the thing finished'?"

"Confustication, Potato. I do wish you would stop objecting to the plot. Of course I do not suggest the four scents will be out there waving banners of welcome for you, but for the love of bacon, I know you know smells. Follow your nose's lead, and stop pretending you aren't brilliant enough to work out what to do with olfactory intelligence as it comes across your nostrils."

"It is true, as you say," said Hercules Potato, conciliated by this appeal to his intelligence, "I have the mind most brilliant. For instance, I am sharp enough to notice your particular use of pronouns." He sat back up on his haunches and stared pointedly down at the Colonel. "Why, Colonel, is it you persist in speaking of this Four-Point Plan, as you call it, with the use of the word 'you'? Do you not mean to say instead, 'we,' that we, you and I, must follow this Four-Point Plan in order to locate the true hero of the lost princess."

The Colonel raised himself up gingerly as he said regretfully, "I would go with you, Potato, with all of my heart I would go with you. I long to go with you, I do hope you understand, but my arthritis prevents it. My poor old legs would not get me even as far as the first scent before they failed me completely. No, no, I shan't be able to journey with you."

"Jappe, jappe, jappe," barked Hercules Potato in protest, "you expect me to go after these scents alone? Always, a famed detective must have by his side an assistant. I am not different in this respect."

"Don't be daft, Potato, I quite understand these things. I have taken the liberty of making the proper arrangements. Even before I came to see you this morning, I had enlisted a young recruit to go along with you."

Now, a new horror presented itself to Hercules Potato's imagination. "Colonel," he swallowed aghast, "you do not mean Pookie Shams?"

A pained expression crossed the Colonel's face. "Potato, you wound me. No, of course I do not mean the Shams bumbler. He's an all right lad I suppose, but I know full well he isn't up to scratch. Good. You go along home and wait for me there. I will go and collect the recruit. I won't be long. You need to get started 'ere the sun is overhead, else you might not find the true hero before dark."

AFTER ALL HAD BEEN DECIDED upon, Hercules Potato took his leave of the Colonel and the Princess Anastazia and headed off home for a brief respite before the case began in earnest. As he went, he passed by the house a few doors up from the home of the hero Jeffries. This house belonged to the curiosity Blevins. Curiosities were so called by dogs for their unaccountable tendency to allow cats into their homes.

"One of life's riddles wrapped in mystery inside of enigmas," the Colonel always said about them. While Hercules Potato endeavoured to keep an open mind about cats generally, this cat in particular disgruntled his tranquility to no small extent. The extreme idea of offering up one's home as a safe harbour to this cat—well, he thought it beggared belief to say the least.

The curiosity Blevins, always the model of politeness when she spoke to Hercules Potato, nonetheless blotted her appeal by her recently formed and close association with this particularly mendacious and very shady Tabby cat called MissTree. Mrs. Blevins, it may be remembered, was off on her cruise round the world, and she had entrusted the feeding and watering of this cat to the grand hero Gwendolyn.

It was painful to picture his hero putting herself to any trouble over so shady a Tabby cat. At least, he thought, the petite heroes were allergic to cats, which meant MissTree would not be allowed admittance to Little Marchmain, however long her curiosity kept away from home. All the same, it rankled.

Hercules Potato tried not to dwell on these things as he went by the house, but mid-trot, he halted abruptly. His spine went rigid, his nose shot upwards towards the bows of the maple tree branching out high above his head. The scent that snared him, wound its way through his olfactory cavities, hissed past his little yellow mucus cells, and wriggled snake-like into his recognition. How well he knew the smell. Then, he heard the sound, a sound ever as welcome to a dog as children welcome influenza on Christmas morning: "Meow."

The famed detective cringed, but remembering his manners, he said, *"Bonjour, mam'zelle* MissTree. Please allow me to offer you my condolences on the going away of your curiosity on the sea cruise."

"If you mean the Blevins creature, I think nothing of he-rrr, whether she goes or stays, as long as I have what I need."

"Ah yes, my hero, she—"

"Out for a pe-rrrrr-ambulation are you, Potato?"

"Oui, c'est vrai, I enjoy the promenade on this most lovely morning, and you? I see that you enjoy the tree, *n'est-ce pas?"* He could just make out her shifty green, feline eyes peering down through the leaves of a branch above him.

"Pe-rrrr-fectly, Potato, I see everything pe-rrrr-fectly from this pe-rrrrr-ch of mine."

"I am sure it is so, *mam'zelle* MissTree, but now, if you will please to excuse me," he said, preparing to go on, "I must be on my way—"

"Pu-rrrr-suing something are you? I know it cannot be a rrr-at you chase, don't I now?"

Hercules Potato started. MissTree smoothly pressed her advantage and in a sweetly smiling voice said, "Oh, does that upset you, Potato? Of course, I know all about your little discomfitu-rrrr-e, don't I now? I also know you are not out here to pe-rrrr-petrate an innocent little walk."

Hercules Potato would have preferred to take his leave here and now, but it would mean leaving this shady Tabby cat with an easily won upper paw, so he cobbled together his stressed nerves and said, "The exercise, it is healthy for me, and if I am also able to accomplish any duty by it, so much the better."

"Duty is just another-rrr word for folly. Cats unde-rrrr-stand there is no such thing as a duty to anyone, except in that one owes a duty to oneself to be happy, to only do what it pleases one to do and to do nothing else besides. Pleasu-rrr-e, Potato, it is all that is real, isn't it now."

"Long ago, *mam'zelle* MissTree, in the far away place which was called Cyrene, there lived a hero philosopher called Aristippus, and he thought much as you do. He would have agreed with the supreme place of honour in which you place what you call the happiness. *Moi*, I do not do not agree. To concern myself solely with my own happiness might too often bring misery to others. I think it is not the good way to live. Now, if you will excuse—"

"You are involved with a lost princess, pe-rrrr-chance?"

He had been once again in mid-trot, and once again he halted abruptly. What answer should he give to this? The Colonel had made a big show out of wanting to keep the princess a secret, but what was the point of hiding it now, if MissTree seemed to know all about it? What would be the harm in confirming it to her?

Then again, harm always lurked behind corners when one said anything to MissTree. One never knew what motivations she held back. Her reason for withholding anything inevitably turned on her insatiable desire to throw a spanner into the works whenever she sensed a dog had a game apaw. However, if he told her noth-ing, he risked her taking an even more unhealthy interest in the matter. Hercules Potato swayed with indecision.

"I saw her you know," crooned the very shady Tabby cat.

45

Hercules Potato stopped swaying. He looked up sharply. "You saw her?

"I watched from a thicket as she came into the glen, and I followed your lost princess all the way as she pe-rrrr-ambulated into Dale-on-Tweedy-Down with the dullard Jeffries, didn't I now?"

"Ah," said Hercules Potato, his ears on the prick, "but that is most wonderful, *mam'zelle* MissTree. Please to tell me, from which direction did she enter into the glen?"

With a self-satisfied little humming, she said, "I am not going to tell you, am I now?"

"*Quoi,* why not? It is most important that you tell to me this information, *mam'zelle* MissTree. You might save us much of the time wasted."

"That is just why I will not tell you. It would spoil my own fun, and you know I would neve-rrrr do that. I will be so happy watching you running around like a pe-rrrr-fect numpty, not knowing where to go next."

"You beastly, ill-mannered feline," shouted Hercules Potato, giving full vent to his contempt of her words.

MissTree shifted slightly on her branch and demurely crossed one paw over the other as she said, "Tut, tut, He-rrrr-cules Potato. It is not nice to call others names. It is a beastly thing to do, isn't it now?"

Hercules Potato sputtered out, "You cannot expect me to be nice to you when you are being the absolute, the most horrible, the most complete epitome of what is said about a cat."

This full throttled condemnation of her species did not faze MissTree in the least. She laughed and said, "You can kick your paws at the sky all you want, He-rrrr-cules Potato, but you will not scratch it. No, you will not. I am a cat, a-rrrr-en't I? Have I not just explained to you we cats never do anything if it does not make us happy to do it? Conversely then, you must unde-rrrr-stand, if it will make us happy to do something, then that is the only thing we shall do."

"*Alors*, it matters not as I am sure you are telling the fibs. I am most certain you saw nothing."

"I know she came here with her vulgar chew toy, don't I now?"

In goading her on in this loathsome conversation, Hercules Potato had managed to hear two things that interested him very much. "Enough," he said, now believing he could extricate himself from the exchange with a small sense of having won something. "This conversation most deplorable has in fact been instructional, and I hope, *mam'zelle* MissTree, you will not find yourself stuck up in this tree should you decide to descend it. That would not, I think, give to you the happiness. *Au revoir.*"

He strutted away with his head and tail held high, the malicious meow from aloft the tree him disturbed him not a wit.

HERCULES POTATO TRAMMELED BACK through the Portuguese laurel and went up to rest on the front porch. As the sun reached its mid point in the sky, the Portuguese laurel next presented the Colonel into the front garden.

"All present and correct I trust?" he said as he came through. "Our young recruit will be along shortly, and the two of you can set off. Good. You know the Four-Point Plan, the four scents: the dead roses, the chickens, the fish, and the chocolates. Should be the easiest case you ever work, Potato."

"I do not share so much confidence as you have, Colonel. I think there is much to go wrong in this Four-Point-Plan. For example, what if we have hunger? There will be no heroes on hand to serve us the dinner."

"I simply do not know how you get on in life worrying as you do, Potato. See here, it took the princess less than half-a-day's journey to get here. If you leave now, you should hit the bit with the fish just about the time you want a snack. Before it is time for you to have your dinner, you will be back here in the home of your heroes."

Hercules Potato would have pointed out Borzois travel much faster than do Belgian Griffons, but the Colonel barreled on, "About your new recruit, a first rate assistant to be sure. I met this dog by way of the company my heroes keep. They often go visiting at the cluster of houses farther out from the High Street. You know them, the ones called the Derby Villas. Ah, that will be her coming now."

A bright and sporty bark sounded from over the crest of the lane. A compact, energetic Jack Russell Terrier raced into view. Infused with the all of the vim and zeal of youth, she jumped and veritably flew over the front gate, skidding to a halt at the front paws of the famed detective.

"Hercules Potato," said the Colonel, "allow me to introduce you to Tess of the Derby Villas." His new, bright and sporty assistant sniffed at Hercules Potato's collar. A small dog herself, she nonetheless stood farther from the ground than he did. Her smart white coat, with its characteristic tawny brown patches, was clean and well groomed, and she wore a little red ribbon tied in a bow at the back of her collar.

Hercules Potato bowed his head gallantly to her and said, *"Je suis enchanté de vous rencontrer, mademoiselle* Tess, it will be an honour most true to have your assistance in this case."

"I'm a fair way to feeling honoured myself," she said. "By the way, I do hope you are going tell me the inside skinny on the arsenic and scent of old lace case. I promised my friend Prufrock I would deliver the goods on it. Poor old Pruie, she's a rather dejected modernist Beagle, and her hero is ill, so neither of them gets out much. It will do her no end of good to hear something peppy from you."

"*Ah oui*, this case you mention, it captured the public imagination in a way that surprises me still," said the famed detective as he sat back on his haunches to reminisce. "It was the case *très simple*, though. As I was accompanying one of my heroes for *une promenade*, I began to sniff the distinctive scent of old lace. I knew it must actually be incredibly old lace because of the scent of the arsenic that I smelled mixed in with it. In former times, you see, some chemist heroes discovered that if they mixed arsenic into the dye of the fabric, they could obtain a brilliant shade of green. Everyone used to marvel at the beauty of such a colour. Unfortunately, the arsenic in the dye caused terrible things to happen to the skin of the worker heroes who made it, as well as to the skin of the customer heroes who wore the clothing made from it."

"Yes, I have heard that chemist heroes have been known to come up with some fairly frightful inventions from time to time," said Tess of the Derby Villas.

"Just as you say, *mam'zelle* Tess. When my hero and I came around the corner, I saw a beautiful *madame* hero wearing a lace shawl in the telltale green shade." Hercules Potato saw that Tess of the Derby Villas was listening with rapt attention, always an encouraging sign to see in a new assistant, he thought.

He went on, "When she sat down on a nearby bench, I ran over to see her up close, and sure enough, there were the beginnings of what must have been for her painful scabbing on her arms and hands. *Moi*, I began to bark at her, and to grab away from her the shawl. This drew the attention of a several other nearby heroes, and one of them, it transpired, also knew of the danger in the green lace and explained to her that she must not touch it anymore."

"Bit of luck for her you were there to step in," said the new bright and sporty assistant.

"*Oui d'accord, mam'zelle* Tess. As it turned out, the *madame* hero had found the old lace shawl in the attic of a house once belonging to her great, great grandmother hero. The old lace shawl is now on display at the Dale-on-Tweedy-Down library, beneath a protective glass case, of course. It bears the heading, "Dressed for Death."

"Brilliant," said Tess of the Derby Villas. "That ought to be just the thing to clear up old Pruie's chronic, existential flu. She is quite impossible most times. Do you know what she said when I told her the Colonel assigned me to assist you to find the true hero of a lost dog?"

"*Mais non*, what is it that she said?"

"She said, what with reality being an elusive un-thing, and truth being unknowable and impossible to communicate even if it could be known, we weren't likely to do any good, and probably, we'd come to a sticky end."

"She takes a grim view of the case, *mam'zelle* Tess."

"Oh well, don't pay any attention to her nonsense. I never do, except to tell her she's potty."

The Colonel, who had by this time begun to pace impatiently to and fro, interjected with an acute, "Ahem." Hercules Potato and Tess of the Derby Villas both turned to him with startled faces that suggested they had rather forgotten he was there. "Enough of the pleasantries," said the Colonel. "The day is getting away from you. Derby Villa here is up to speed on the four point plan, but there is one more thing that may be of use to you."

He went back to the Portuguese laurel and reached his muzzle into it. He pulled out what Hercules Potato recognised with surprise as the royal chew toy of the Princess Anastazia. "It occurred to me," explained the Colonel, "if you can present this royal chew toy at the palace, it will be all the easier for you to make it understood that you come with tidings from the lost princess."

Tess of the Derby Villas leaned down to give it a thorough sniffing, while Hercules Potato said, "*Très bien*, Colonel, you impress me. I had the same idea myself, *bien sûr*, but I did not like to mention it to the princess. She might have fired me on the spot." Although, he judged privately, it would have been a convenient way to get out of what he was more and more convinced would become an arduous case.

"I myself had a deuce of a time convincing the Princess Anastazia to part with it, but I made her see reason in the end. I gave her my word of honour, mind you, that you will not lose it. So don't."

"*Merci*, Colonel," said Hercules Potato. "We will not mar your honour by such carelessness. The royal chew toy will be delivered safely to the palace." Then he turned to his bright and sporty assistant and said, "*Alors, mam'zelle* Tess, you will please to carry the chew toy in your teeth?"

"Me?" asked Tess of the Derby Villas. "Dash it, why do I have to carry it? How do you expect me to chase and sniff and run down scents with that ruddy thing in my mouth all the while? I might as well trot off on the adventure wearing high heeled shoes."

"*Ma foi*, surely you do not expect that I, Hercules Potato, should be the one to carry such a thing?" An expectation of this kind was not an encouraging sign in a new assistant, and the famed detective began to have his doubts about her.

"Let's not have a mutiny before you either of you leave the front garden," said the Colonel. "If you had waited but half a minute to start rowing about it, you would have seen that I come prepared for this controversy." He returned his muzzle into the hedge, and this time he pulled out a brightly coloured, cloth sack. "The royal chew toy is to be carried in this sack. I borrowed it from one of my heroes. She makes things like this with her own ten fingers; it is most impressive. I think you will find, Derby Villa, the strap attached to it is just the right length to slip around your collar and not be a bother to you while you run and sniff and do all your commission requires of you."

Tess of the Derby Villas sniffed the brightly coloured sack, and then said, "Jolly reasonable, I can get along fine with this version of the scheme." She pushed the royal chew toy into the sack with her nose, while the Colonel held it open with his teeth. Then, she lowered her head, and the Colonel, still using his teeth, pulled the strap over her ears and adjusted it around her collar. It rested just in front her breastbone, and while it would no doubt flap around a little, such annoyance would not be terribly noticeable to her.

"So," said the Colonel, "that's that and time you were off."

"Three cheers for us, and let's start the show going," agreed Tess of the Derby Villas. The trio of dogs filed back through the Portuguese laurel and onto the pavement along the lane. The Colonel turned to the two departing dogs and said, "My Four-Point Plan is as sound a thing as you could need. I will just pop over tomorrow, Potato, and you can give me a full report. What a thing it would be for me to go with you myself. You are going to have the time your lives, I shouldn't wonder."

Tess of the Derby Villas nodded her head and said brightly, "Rightio, Colonel, toodle-pip."

Hercules Potato slid his eyes warily in the Colonel's direction, but he only said, "*Au revoir*, Colonel."

They started up the lane towards the crest of the small hill, where the lane joined the High Street. The Colonel crossed over to his own front garden and watched them go off until they disappeared. Then, he too disappeared into his house, and the sun shone down upon an empty scene. As Tess of the Derby Villas would later tell her friend Prufrock, "It was a splendid beginning to an arduous case destined to go belly-up before one could say, 'peevish princess.'"

~

CHAPTER IV

THE SCENT OF THE DEAD ROSES

*T*he two small dogs crossed the High Street and descended to the other side of the hill. From there, they made their way to the lane leading northwards towards the glen where the hero Jeffries found the princess the day before. As they passed the gate guarding the entrance to the old pile called

Plummley Hall, they heard a voice carrying deep and wide from atop the hill. It called out, "Ee – pim – o – nee." The voice belonged to the hero Sir Wordsworth Plumm, previously alluded to as the grand hero Gavin's nemesis in all things pertaining to front gardens.

Hercules Potato stopped and watched while a Frisbee breezed across the hilltop, and the graceful figure of a Hungarian Vizsla lept up to catch it. As she ran the distance back towards her hero, a second graceful figure joined her in the race. Beyond them, could be seen the grey stone turrets of Plummley Hall contrasting against the soft blue of the spring sky, but it was the sight of the dogs that entranced Hercules Potato. He lingered in his spot, marvelling at this pair of highly esteemed Hungarian Vizslas, Cassius and Epimone.

They glided across the hilltop, their muzzles noble, their legs long and lean, their caramel coloured bodies arching and contracting in perfect rhythm and graceful form. Indeed, the enthralling sight of Cassius and Epimone in motion together always called to the famed detective's mind a fleeting vision of the long disappeared, magnificent grandeur of the Austro-Hungarian Empire.

Hercules Potato, generally speaking, felt happy to be himself, a Belgian Griffon, and a famed detective. What he lacked in height, he trusted he made up for with intelligence, skill, and a proper respect for the seriousness of life. Still, he did ofttimes lament his short legs, his diminutive stature, and his lack of any sort of jaw line.

He heard the occasional remarks of others who said things to his heroes along the lines of, "He is a small one, does he actually have any legs?" He had also heard it said of him, "He'll do as company for the children, but a dog will need to have more of a jaw than he's got if you want to keep the rats out." Worse, was how often the dreadful word, "cute," seemed to get bandied about whenever he made the acquaintance of a new hero. "Oh isn't he just the cutest little bittykins who ever tried to bark," said one such commentator. The bitterness of that moment still clung to his put-upon soul.

Hercules Potato had always been a dog to appreciate beauty, but he inwardly admitted he did not exactly see beauty's example when he inspected himself in reflective surfaces. He felt this self-doubt most acutely whenever he saw Cassius and Epimone, both of whom he held up as highly esteemed examples of beauty. How must it feel, he wondered, to be so beautiful, to be so tall, and to have such wonderfully defined jaw lines?

"Gudgeons and gingercakes," said Tess of the Derby Villas. "What are you staring at Potato? We don't have all year, you know."

Hercules Potato shook himself out with vigour and called as he started briskly towards her, "Quite correct, *mam'zelle* Tess. The sight of the beauty, it arrests my soul, but it does not pause the daylight. *Nous y allons.*"

They made quick work reaching the part of the glen where the brook widened along a soft, mossy bank, and the trees graciously shaded a well-used towpath. They supposed from all they knew, it was in this general area where the hero Jeffries found the Princess Anastazia. They began sniffing about, and quite soon, Hercules Potato said, "We are in the location correct, *mam'zelle* Tess, for I smell the scent of the princess distinctly here."

"Her toffee-nosed highness makes herself duly noticed, I agree, but dash it, I don't smell any dead roses, do you, Potato?"

"*Non*, I detect nothing of the dead roses. *Zut alors*, the cat, MissTree, she knows where exactly we must go, but would she tell me? *Non*, she would not."

"Just as well, Potato. Ever since she came to Dale-on-Tweedy-Down, that shady tabby cat hasn't spoken a line of anything if it wasn't a porky pie. Anything she might have told you is bound to be dodgy information."

Hercules Potato said, "We must stop for a moment, *mam'zelle* Tess. I must sit and consult with the logic."

As he sat, he pondered the Colonel's Four-Point Plan. Finding the scent of the dead roses had always seemed to him to be the plan's weakest point. Granted, it sounded nicely artistic to say that one searches for the scent of dead roses, but it did not offer any tangible meaning to enlighten one's path. Vague, abstract concepts, he considered, flew in the face of a detective who worked purely on the strength of the scents and the logic.

To be sure, the success of all the other points in the plan hinged upon finding this mercurial first scent, the dead roses. He felt inclined to agree with the friend of *mam'zelle* Tess, the dejected, modernist beagle Prufrock, and her doomed-to-failure assessment of the case.

"MissTree," he murmured under his breath. There is something there in what she told to me, he thought to himself. The two things I noticed she said, what do they mean here? He murmured again, "I know she came here with her chew toy." It is one of the things she said to me. *Ah oui*, of course. He said, "*Mam'zelle* Tess, stop sniffing just now for the dead roses. It is a scent better left to the poets to worry over. What we must find now is the trail smelling of the Princess Anastazia and of the cat MissTree together. When we find it, we will know where to go."

"I don't know, Potato," she said. "It mightn't be a corking idea to abandon the Four-Point Plan so soon and all because of some rubbish MissTree purred on about."

"That is quite well and good, *mam'zelle* Tess, and for a beginner such as yourself, it would be wise to stick to the plan previously decided upon. I, however, am the famed detective. I am able to improvise because I am more advanced in understanding the course of an investigation. What is more, the Colonel, he did not have this information when he suggested this plan of his. I discovered it when I interrogated the cat MissTree myself."

He moved closer to her, whispering his next few words. "I

have it from the cat herself that she followed the princess for some distance before the hero Jefferies found her."

The sound of a twig breaking in the distance made his assistant whisper as well, as she said, "If it is true, it might be vital information, Potato. I don't like it though. It's ten stones more likely, being the determined fibster she is, that MissTree told you a tale as tall as fir trees."

Hercules Potato shook his head. "I know she likes to tell the fibs, but she let slip some information proving her story to be true, which I am sure she did not mean to do. No matter, this is information I think the Colonel, if he were here, would say calls for the retrenching of the plan."

"All right, assuming it's as true as bacon, what did she tell you?"

Still whispering, he said, "The Tabby cat most shady, she told to me that while she was lurking in a thicket somewhere, she saw the princess carry with her the royal chew toy as she wandered into this this glen. If MissTree had not been following her, she could not know this fact of the chew toy's existence. *Donc*, we must search for where the scent of the cat and the scent of the princess go *tous les deux* in the same direction. This will help to lead us to where the scent of the princess, it goes on alone."

"Well, it's your show, old boy, you are the jolly good detective after all. If that's where you want to take the script, I shall defer to you."

"But of course, *mam'zelle* Tess, I am the jolly good detective, it is as you say. *Alors*, if we trace the points where the scent of the cat and the scent of the princess go along together, maybe we might even discover the scent of the dead roses."

"That's a sensible bit of thinking, Potato, but I say, before we get on with it, might we hit up that brook over there for a drink of water?"

"Ah *oui*, *mam'zelle* Tess, I too feel in need of refreshment."

So, fatigued and thirsty, the two dogs lapped up the delicious water from the brook and rested for a short time on the soft, mossy bank. Later, Tess of the Derby Villas would tell her friend Prufrock, "After that, we went on with the agreed upon program, still with the naive idea we would be back in time to feed from the home-front dinner pail at the usual hour."

∾

ALL AFTERNOON, they sniffed hither and thither. They smelled living leaves on trees and dead leaves on the ground. They sniffed squirrels and the scent of sweat left by recent jogger heroes. Here, they sniffed out a wet sock; there, they came nose-to-feather with a deceased bird. At long length, they found the lingering scent of the cat MissTree in a thicket of newly trampled foliage.

They barked joyfully and congratulated each other merrily on achieving a definitive success at last. To their delight, they found it did indeed track behind the scent of the princess, and following the two scents took them well out of the glen and away from Dale-on-Tweedy-Down. They made slow progress because they went along a rough, unknown path, chocked with brambles.

Meanwhile, the sun slipped ever farther across its own quite familiar path down towards the horizon.

At last, the thicket cleared and their path became easier. Tess of the Derby Villas said, "MissTree's scent is getting to be a bit thin on the ground, and I say, have you detected a few new scents creeping in? I can't quite put my paw on what they might be."

She observed Hercules Potato in a still pose, deep in concentration, his nose hovering just above the ground. "What is it, Potato? What do you smell?"

He sniffed a few more times, thoughtfully and silently, before he said, "These new scents, *mam'zelle* Tess, I fear they foretell of something we approach that is most sad."

Tess of the Derby Villas' eyes became large circles of deep brown concern. Her head cocked sideways and she waited for him to continue.

He rose to all fours and said, "I smell the scent of many yew trees, and I smell other mournful scents as they rise from deep beneath the ground. Also, there is another mysterious scent that is as yet unfamiliar to me. They all lead in the same direction."

"Yew trees?

"*Oui*, the yew trees, and the something else often associated with them," the famed detective almost whispered, "*Le source de larmes.*"

"What's that you said?"

"The source of tears, *mam'zelle* Tess. For with the scent of these yew trees there is also the scent of the bones of heroes."

Tess of the Derby Villas drooped her head as he went on with his deduction. "I perceive from what I smell that there is a graveyard not far off. When we come through this thicket, we will probably be able to see it. Knowing this much, I am also willing to risk a guess and to say we shall find there the scent of the dead roses."

Tess of the Derby Villas perked up at this and said, "I say, but it all makes sense now. The princess must have come from the graveyard when she wandered into this loathsome thicket and got spotted by MissTree."

"I smell no more of the cat MissTree, and I agree with you, the scent of the Princess Anastazia, it goes in the direction of this graveyard, but as I said, there is another scent that I cannot yet identify. In any case, it will be a relief to be out of the thicket so troublesome. We are close. We begin to close in on the first scent, *mam'zelle* Tess. *Nous y allons.*"

The two dogs forged on and came through to a clearing. A road stretched out in front of them, and on the other side of it, they saw a low stonewall. This parted at an entrance over which hung a high iron arch. The entrance did not have a gate, so the two dogs entered under it without hindrance.

"This dreary place, *mam'zelle* Tess, it reminds me of a line spoken by the hero poet Dante as he came near to the Dolorous City. 'The Day departs, and the brown air takes the animals on the earth from their toils.'"

"I say, but you are dishing up some rather glum stuff, Potato. Wasn't there a well that led down to Hades in that story? Oh don't let's think about it. A dog could do with some food just about now though."

Even after they entered the graveyard, the scent of the dead roses never became very much. As they passed one after another rounded, stone slab, they eventually saw a few dead roses lying here and there. Other sorts of dried and dead flowers were scattered about as well, and even a few freshly picked flowers appeared in spots.

The tangled and time-sculpted trunks of the yew trees drifted silently upwards, spreading out their willowy limbs one to another, forming dark green canopies over the stillness below. A somber hush permeated all things in this place. One cannot be lively or spirited in a place where not even the martins flutter or sing. No petite heroes played here. Grand heroes did not appear around corners here. There were no balls, no laughter, no whis-tled tunes.

Hercules Potato breathed in and smelled a heavy scent creeping up from below ground. Bones. The bones of heroes lay deep beneath this ground. Lost heroes. Lost, lamented heroes no dog would ever find again. He remembered the Colonel's words, "Only death is permitted to sever dog from hero for the rest of time."

He bowed his head and whispered, "The source of every tear, it is indeed found here."

A far away trace of evensong floated in with the last daylight breezes. The yew trees rustled and shifted their branches, and high above them, the waning warmth of the sun, low in the western sky, gave way to a dusky chill.

Hercules Potato cast a forlorn glance at the sinking sun and said, "*Mam'zelle* Tess, Phoebus, he now yawns and is ready for sleep. He will give us no more light today."

"It doesn't bode well for the Colonel's simple, Four-Point Plan. I don't recall him proposing an overnight stay under a tree, much less an overnight stay under a tree in a graveyard."

"It is not the arrangement most ideal," said Hercules Potato, "but we can trust to the logic, *n'est-ce pas?* It cannot be that sleeping under a tree in a graveyard is any different from sleeping under a tree in any other place."

Tess of the Derby Villas returned him doubtful expression. A spasmodic shiver came over her from tail to muzzle. She timidly lowered her nose towards the ground, hesitating before she sniffed. Her sense of smell guided her to a soft mound of grass, tucked behind a stone slab, a few paces from the trunk of a yew tree. Hercules Potato followed behind, and helped her to slide the sack from around her neck. She placed it in between herself and the stone slab as a sort of cushion.

As she lay down, she said, "My little bed in the Derby Villas seems far away and wonderful just about now."

An owl hooted just above them, hastening a startled Hercules Potato to curl up next to her. Light and shadow faded fully away. Hanging above the darkness, the crescent moon allowed them only just enough light to trace the tops of the stone slabs spread out around them.

Hercules Potato's stomach growled. In an effort to not think about food, he asked, "Did you meet the so called Princess Anastazia, *mam'zelle* Tess?"

Yawning, she said, "Oh yes, I met her nibs early this morning. She is the dog of a hundred Czars that one, except it seems she doesn't know how to cope with poultry when it is set before her in a live condition. Fancy the likes of her taking fright from a few chickens." She yawned again. "I cannot work it out at all."

"Ah *oui*, I thought this too, *mam'zelle* Tess. How is it a dog so magnificent, even one so impossible as this Borzoi, could be reduced to trembling terror by some pesky little chickens?"

Tess of the Derby Villas muttered as she began drifting off to sleep, "Too much cossetting from her hero I expect. She's gone and gotten soft."

Hercules Potato listened as her breathing took on the soft and regular rhythm of sleep. Alone in his wakefulness with the gaping expanse of the night, he shivered and waited for sleep to take him off to some pleasant dream, perhaps of the Lady Stella. Even if one is unswervingly logical, a graveyard is a lonely arena, filled only with those who are gone. Gone forever. However much one might cling to logic and insist it is just a place like any other, an oppressive heaviness hangs about its atmosphere. Strong in the undercurrent of thought is the whispering dread of yet more who are loved being lost here one day.

Hercules Potato shivered again and moved a little closer to the sleeping Tess of the Derby Villas. As his stomach continued to growl, he felt a slight tinge of resentment of the Colonel for assuring him the Four-Point Plan would bring them back home tonight. Ah, home. Hercules Potato thought of his lovely kitchen cushion, of the smell of bacon sizzling on the Aga stove, of the placid tones of the grand hero Gavin and of the firm but kind voice of the grand hero Gwendolyn, whose love of the rules and the proper order of things equaled his own.

He thought of the petite heroes, of how wonderful they were. So ready to run around the back garden with him, to accompany him for walks, and always reliable when it came to ensuring at least some little bits of the best parts of every meal fell to the floor. He even had a kind thought or two about Pookie Shams, who, despite his many flaws, could always be counted on to be cheerful.

He thought of the Lady Stella. All of his present discomfort melted away in the vision of her that appeared in his heart. As the glooming scent of the Yew trees lay heavily overhead, he closed his eyes and remembered her far-off enchanting scent. He thought of her silk and satin voice, and of the glittering brown of her eyes. His lids became heavy, and he drifted into a sleep that relieved him of all his present discomforts. As he closed his own eyes, he did not know that another pair of eyes stalked towards the graveyard in search of him. He did not know that these eyes would find him.

THE HEROES at the fifth house on the left, the one with the tree swing in the front garden, did not at first notice Hercules Potato's absence from Little Marchmain when they all returned home in the late afternoon. It was by no means an unusual event for the small dog to take himself off on some hidden business. They could at any rate, always count on the dinner hour to result in his prompt reappearance in the kitchen.

After everyone had their tea and went off to pursue their separate interests, the grand hero Gwendolyn, unaware anything was amiss in her own home, had gone over to her neighbour's home.

She called out, "Miss Flea, are you here?" but the cat, if it was there, declined to show herself.

The grand hero Gwendolyn left behind a clean litter box and full bowls of water and food. Returning to her own kitchen, she nestled herself into a cozy nook. Pookie Shams observed her perusing her cookbook, while glancing up from time to time at a program on the B. W. S. (Incidentally, that stands for the Box Without Smells, and it quite bewilders dogs, who cannot think why heroes should spend so much time in front of an object that offers no olfactory interest.)

Pookie Shams inspected her position, sniffed at her ankles, waited while she patted his head, then he trotted off upstairs. There, he located the petite hero Lewis ensconced in the book room. Once again, a few sniffs were all he needed to ascertain he was not needed in that corner of the world. He then took himself back down the stairs, through the hall passage, back through the kitchen, and out through the dog's door.

Rounding a back corner, he located the grand hero Gavin and the petite hero Montcy deep in conference over a task occupying them at the side of the house.

"Well now," said the grand hero Gavin as Pookie Shams came up and licked his elbow, "I'd say that just about does it, Montcy. All we need to finish things is to program the command to set off the sprinklers with a secret code word. That way, I don't need to fumble around in the bushes for the button every time I want to water the front garden. When I am away from home, you can come back here, say the code word yourself, and all will be well and watered."

Montcy nodded her head and asked, "Can I turn it off just the same way?"

"In theory, yes, it should turn off when you say the code word, the same as it turns it on," he answered, but scratching his head he explained, "except I have not been able to work out those instructions yet. So, meantime, just don't forget that after about an hour or so, you will need to reach down here and turn it off manually. It is just as bad for a garden to be over-watered as under-watered."

"I know, Daddy, I won't forget. Pookie Shams will help me to remember." She sat down on the grass and took the little white dog into her lap.

The grand hero Gavin asked, "What code word should we choose, do you think?"

"Rozie Ratzo," replied the petite hero without a moment's hesitation.

"Rozie Ratzo, you say. Who is she, dear one?"

"She is an international spy."

"Oh," exclaimed the grand hero, more than a bit surprised. "Where did you come across her?"

"In my book at school, Rozie Ratzo Saves the Queen."

"Oh, I see, I see. A spy you say? A rat you say? No one much likes either particularly well I should think, bit too sneaky for most."

"Rozie Ratzo is not a sneak, and since she is a spy, it makes her name perfect as a secret code word for the sprinkler," defended the petite hero a bit huffily, before she added nobly, "She does everything for Queen and country."

"For what?" asked the grand hero Gavin, "It all sounds a right lot of propaganda to me, though I dare say your mother would lap it up with delight."

"Propa- what?" queried the petite hero.

"Oh well, never mind what it is," said the grand hero as he steered the conversation back to the intended point. "It says here, dear one, the word we choose must be no more than three letters. I am afraid that sneak or no, it leaves Rozie Ratzo quite out of the running as a secret code word for our sprinkler."

The petite hero Montcy, however, would not be deterred so easily. She said, "We could just pick rat. R-A-T, that's a three letter word."

"So it is," said the grand hero Gavin, "Six years old and clever to boot, my Montcy. Rat it shall be." He set to programing the agreed upon secret code word into the system, while Pookie Shams gave an approving bark and licked the back of the petite hero's hand.

Some while later, everyone noticed that Hercules Potato failed to put in an appearance at the appointed dinner hour, and it was then that concern over him came to the fore. The front garden rang out with the calls of "Hercules Potato, where are you?"

"Hercules Potato, here old fellow. Come on home, fellow."

"Hercules Potato, come and get your dinner."

Their calls attracted the Airedale who lived across the lane, and he came running over to sniff expectantly around them, but where was Hercules Potato? The grand hero Gavin's whistle cut a high-pitched summons through the darkening lane, but it failed to produce Hercules Potato for inspection. The petite heroes were terribly glum at the dinner table and barely tasted their food. Pookie Shams too looked saddened. He even abstained from eating the food in Hercules Potato's bowl. Everyone missed the Belgian Griffon terribly. The petite hero Montcy began to cry.

"Don't cry, my darling," comforted her mother. "Let's hope he will come home tomorrow." She put her arm around her child and pulled her tightly against her.

"But what if he is lost and can't find his way back?" asked the petite hero Lewis.

"Then maybe some kind stranger will find him and call us," answered the grand hero Gavin. "He is wearing his collar and tags, you know, and it is reasonable to think tomorrow will deliver him back to us."

"No," objected the petite hero Montcy through her sobs. "No, I think he ran away."

"Oh," exclaimed the grand hero Gwendolyn. "Why would he do that, dearest? Hercules Potato loves it here with us. This is his home, and I don't think he would run away. Dogs are not prone to exchange perfect comfort in a home for unknown hardship out in the wild. I shouldn't think it at all in his nature to do such a thing."

"I yelled him, that's why," the petite hero Montcy confessed. "I yelled at him this morning, because he was barking at Pookie Shams, and I said, 'No, Hercules Potato, stop being a bully boss, and let Pookie Shams alone.'" She said mournfully and finished, "I think I hurt his feelings. I didn't mean to, but I think he got upset. So he left us."

Pookie Shams, though routinely accused by Hercules Potato of being an unperceptive dog, nonetheless pattered forward and licked the petite hero's small kneecap. He lay down at her feet to make his show of support complete. The grand hero Gavin offered her some consolation as well, saying, "I do think, dear one, Hercules Potato knows that you love him. This business about hurt feelings is a lot of nonsense. Our Hercules Potato is made of better stuff than to act the coward by running away without saying goodbye."

"Yes, I quite agree with your father, he would never do anything half so selfish," affirmed the grand hero Gwendolyn, wiping her daughters tears away with a dinner napkin.

"Then too, he wasn't mad at me," said the petite hero Lewis. "He would have stayed here to be with me, even if he doesn't like you anymore, Montcy."

The grand hero Gavin coughed disapprovingly at his son. "Eh, my boy, that's not the best stuff to say just at the moment. What we need is to rally round the family."

He turned back to the petite hero Montcy and said, "Now please don't worry, dear one. If Hercules Potato were here right now, and even if he was upset with you, he would come into this room and forgive you with a great big lick on your face. So, let's end all this tosh that says anyone here did anything to make him leave. We will all go to bed, and when we wake up tomorrow, we can start making some signs and start asking around the village if anyone saw him. That is, assuming he does not come in through the dog's door tonight and surprise us all first thing in the morning when we find him asleep on his kitchen cushion just as we did this morning."

This speech achieved a good effect upon its hearers, and everyone gave Pookie Shams an extra special amount of affection before going upstairs for the night. Left alone in the darkened kitchen, the mixed Poodle-Terrier, who was very good at rats, listened anxiously to every outside noise. He strained his ears in concentration, not wanting to miss the sound of Hercules Potato's paws when they came clicking along the gravel towards the dog's door, but he did not hear the least patter. Pookie Shams whimpered and sighed, and lay his head sadly on Hercules Potato's kitchen cushion. For lonely is the night indeed when it is empty of the one we love.

CHAPTER V

THE NIGHT OF TERROR, AND, ABOUT THOSE CHICKENS

*S*everal hours past midnight, a swift, chilly breeze swept Hercules Potato out of his dream, in which he had been instructing the Lady Stella in the best methods for catching rats. Coming out of sleep, he did not understand where he was, but it was clear he was not stretched out on his kitchen cushion. He sniffed at the sleeping form of Tess of the Derby Villas. This brought his predicament back to him, and he stood up and stretched out his forelegs, then his hind legs.

As he considered the most worthy tree to bless, another chill wind went through him. He circled to the back of the yew tree near where he had been sleeping. As he came back around, he noticed a strange bluish light in the far distance— a trick of the moon perhaps? Its sliver of lunar glow cast a faint pallor over the outlines of row upon row of stone slabs. All continued quiet and still, except his stomach rumbled dreadfully. He could not help but let a mournful whimper escape through his nose.

He looked out again at the bluish light. It had not been stationary. Though at first a considerable distance away, it had begun to gain on him. He heard a gasp behind him.

"Potato, what the deuce is that ghastly bluish thing coming at us?" asked Tess of the Derby Villas as she came along side him.

"*Moi,* I do not know, *mam'zelle* Tess, it is a trick of the moon, *peut-être?*"

"I rather doubt it. Crescent moons don't have enough gusto in them to get up to much trickery. Zounds, but don't you think that bluish orb is getting rather an outline of shape to it now?"

Hercules Potato began to feel himself shivering. He told himself that it was because of the cold night air, and not from any sense of being frightened. He looked at his assistant, whose floppy ears had shot up into two petrified points, and whose eyes were decidedly bulged. A sudden sound of frantic scuffling behind them made both dogs turn rapidly around, but they could not see anything or anyone there.

"That sounded rather like a cat," said Tess of the Derby Villas. She sniffed a few times. "I say, it smells rather like— no, couldn't be." She turned back towards the bluish orb. "Yes, I do believe it is changing shape."

They began to see the unmistakable shape of a glowing, blue dog wafting forwards to meet them. Hercules Potato consulted the scents and the logic for help discovering what it was they were dealing with. Perhaps his trusty methods were still fast asleep, for they sent back to him no information. "The scents and the logic, they give me nothing to go on here. *Mam'zelle* Tess, what do you think is the nature of this blueness that comes towards us?"

"I think it is a ghost dog."

"*Mais non*, this is not possible. It is only the trick of the digestion," he said. "There are no such things as the ghost dogs. The undigested beef and the blots of the mustard, did they not make the hero Ebenezer Scrooge think he saw the dead hero Marley in his bed chamber?"

"Marley, if you will remember, actually was a ghost," said Tess of the Derby Villas. "At any rate, we haven't got bits of beef and mustard in our stomachs, more's the pity."

The dog-like spectre halted mere paces away from the famed detective and his bright and sporty assistant. A deathly cold shaft of tinted blue wind blew icily around them. For a moment, the two living dogs stared out with a mixture of dread and disbelief while fright held them tight to their spot. The rational mind of Hercules Potato again sought counsel from the scents and the logic. Groggily, they reported back that if he cared to pay attention, he might just be able to see in the dog-like spectre some suggestion of a Danish Broholmer.

"*Zut alors, mam'zelle* Tess," he said in disbelief, "it must be a dream."

"Whose dream is it? Yours or mine?"

"*Peut-être*, if we lie down, and we go again to sleep, we will wake from this dream."

"You're talking dashed nonsense, Potato. What's that he's doing now?"

The spectral dog had begun to point with his muzzle in a direction off to the right.

"I think, *mam'zelle* Tess, it wants to tell us something." Hercules

Potato took another few cautious steps forwards. The spectral dog again motioned with his muzzle.

"Don't get too close, Potato," his assistant whispered after him, "he could give you lunacy."

"*Mais non*, it is not logical what you say," he said back to her. Clearing his throat and assuming an authoritative tone, he demanded of the spectre, "Who are you?"

The spectral dog did not reply but indicated once more to the right with his muzzle. Tess of the Derby Villas crept up next to Hercules Potato. Another cold, blue wind wound about their ankles, and the yew tree leaves rustled furiously overhead. Now it was she who took a few steps closer the spectre. She sniffed the air, but the spectral Broholmer did not have a scent to him. She followed the famed detective's example and made him a direct address. "Who are you, and what do you want with us?"

The spectral dog gave a deferential bow before he answered her. As he spoke, his frail voice sounded as if it came from far away. "In life, I answered to the name of Thane Mortimer, and in death, I do not forget it."

Hercules Potato again stepped forward to query the spectral dog. "And why do you show yourself to us, Thane Mortimer?"

The spectral dog lowered his head as if from shame, then he answered, "In life, treasure I once buried here remains buried here. A marrow filled, bone of an ox, that is what I buried here, and still here it lies. Long did I persist in saving it, always thinking I must wait until tomorrow to enjoy it. Tomorrow followed after tomorrow, until I reached the one last yesterday which does not give any more tomorrows."

Tess of the Derby Villas scratched her ear and whispered to Hercules Potato, "What's he nuttering on about?"

"I believe, *mam'zelle* Tess," he answered, "the good Thane Mortimer, he speaks of the day on which he died. He saved his bone for so long, he died before he could enjoy it."

"Oh, dashed unfortunate," she said. Turning back to the spectre, she asked, "How long ago was it, Thane Mortimer, when you handed in your dinner pail?"

"Eight nights and one morning past from this night, I could smell and be smelled. Then it last was that I could lick the palm of my hero and feel the touch of her hand upon my brow."

Hercules Potato said, "Your sorrow and the sorrow of your hero at your passing, it is why it is said of death that it is the source of every tear. However, it cannot be good for you to remain in this graveyard as the mere spectre of a once living Danish Broholmer. Thane Mortimer, tell to us why you have not left to find the peace for always that waits for you beyond this place?"

"Because," answered the ghost of Thane Mortimer, "there is a river I must cross before I am permitted to forever lie in peaceful slumber. Those who stand guard upon this river refuse me its passage. They command me to wait here until some living dog will find my lovely, marrow filled ox bone and enjoy it in my place."

Hercules Potato said, "Mm, I have heard of something like this before, but I dismissed it as a myth told to puppies in order to make them behave."

Tess of the Derby Villas whispered into his ear. "I say, Potato, we stand to benefit from this ox bone business."

He quite took her point. The famed detective decided to bring the matter out into the open. He said, "We understand you, Thane Mortimer. It is the River Styx you speak of *n'est-ce pas?*"

Thane Mortimer answered, "Your knowledge well becomes you. Yes, this river is just as you have named it."

"*Donc*, then here we are, *mam'zelle* Tess, and myself, Hercules Potato. We are weary travellers, having much hunger. We will enjoy your bone, if you will please to take us to it, and you, oh good Thane Mortimer, you may cross the River Styx and enjoy the peace final, *d'accord?*

"May it be as you say," answered the ghost of Thane Mortimer.

"I say, as long as we are having a staff meeting," said Tess of the Derby Villas, "you didn't by any chance see a magnificent but impossible Borzoi wandering through here a day or two ago, did you, Mortimer old chap?"

"This dog, I did see," he answered, "but she could not see me. In daylight, it is not permitted to me to be seen. She did not linger here to wait for darkness, but took her way through these grounds dolorous to the lands living while the sun continued to have much discourse with the sky."

"Did you see from which direction the Borzoi entered the graveyard?" asked Hercules Potato.

"I am able to grant this knowledge to you, for I stood over the spot where lies my bone buried when I saw her enter through the gate far and lonely."

"Rather," exclaimed Tess of the Derby Villas, "it hasn't been an unchancy night after all. Take us to your bone, old chap, and we will bid you swift journey over the River Styx. Those blast and wretch guards can get stuffed."

"Follow after me," he called, even then on his way thither. Hercules Potato shot off after him calling back as he went, "*Mam'zelle* Tess, the royal chew toy, do not forget it."

She scurried back around the stone slab and grabbed the vital sack with her teeth, and bounding through the darkness caught up the race. Thane Mortimer led them down a narrow, winding path. He guided them around bleak crypts, and passed with them below stone cut angels and monuments to heroes long since lost to death.

They came to a rounded area, formed by a circle of crumbling stone benches that made a gathering around a dried up, ancient fountain. Here, the ghost of Thane Mortimer paused. Hercules Potato sniffed and scratched at the ground with his paw. "Are we arrived at the spot where you buried your bone of the ox?"

"Yes, ah, yes," he answered mournfully. "Thus did I bury it here." He indicated a portion of ground near the crumbling fountain. "And over there is the gate from whence your Borzoi entered this realm dolorous."

Tess of the Derby Villas shot forward, passing right through the midst of the ghost in her haste to start digging.

"Yes," Thane Mortimer encouraged her. "There is where you must dig. It will not be work done in vain."

Hercules Potato turned to the spectral Broholmer and said, "Thane Mortimer, we thank you. You point us to the nourishment when we are most in need of it, and you point to us to the path of the Borzoi for which we search. The guards at the River Styx, they will assuredly grant to you the right to pass over it now."

"May it be as you express, worthy Hercules Potato," said Thane Mortimer.

A cock crowed in a nearby tree as Tess of the Derby Villas called back from the midst of her digging, "If you wouldn't mind pitching in, Potato, I could use the help."

"*Oui, bien sûr*," he said, as he joined in to dig with her. It took a bit of doing, but they could smell the scent of the marrow, and it drove them to keep digging. They succeeded in unearthing an enormous bone, filled as promised with delicious and nourishing marrow. They chewed, and they gnawed, and they licked until its broken bits were scattered all about them, and no traces of marrow remained. It was not, to be sure, what one could call a satisfying meal, but it took the edge off the worst of their empty stomachs.

Having done all that she could do, Tess of the Derby Villas licked her lips and asked, "Where is Thane Mortimer?"

"He is gone," answered Hercules Potato. "He is gone, and, it is to be hoped, he is crossed to the other side of the River Styx where he may sleep in the peace. We have been of useful service to him and he to us. *Alors*, we must be no longer in this unhappy place, *mam'zelle* Tess. The morning light is soon to arrive, and we have three more scents to follow before the night makes its return. We know our way is through the gate over there."

He helped Tess of the Derby Villas to arrange the sack around her neck, and then they set off down the path leading out of the graveyard, just as it had led the Princess Anastazia into it. As they brushed past a rusted, iron crypt door, Hercules Potato said, "*Mam'zelle Tess*, yesterday the Colonel, he spoke of the death that separated the hero and the dog forever. In this dolorous ground of sorrow, I have felt that here truly is the source of every tear we shed. Then, here too we meet the ghost of a dog who is not yet fully departed. I ask myself whether this power of death to close away from us the heroes whom we love, this barred fast door that causes all of our tears, is it true that it can never be opened again? Is there no way to free all who are locked behind it?"

"Don't let on to old Pruie that I said so, Potato, but it has always been my secret hope that somewhere, there must be a hero who can bust that door down. What do the scents and the logic say about it? "

"Ah, *mam'zelle* Tess, they say it is not their lookout."

They trotted on. The martins, yesterday so quiet, found heart enough in the spreading dawn to sing a little morning song from overhead, while they watched the two dogs depart the dolorous grounds. Shadow and night lifted, and Phoebus striding, took his place in the sky.

HERCULES POTATO and Tess of the Derby Villas passed out of the graveyard and onto a lane running along a wood. The scent of motor oil mixing with tyre rubber did not surprise them, but the famed detective said, "The scent mysterious that puzzled me yesterday, it is here again today. It is at once strange to me and yet somehow also familiar, and I am unable to fix upon what it means."

"I say," put in his bright and sporty assistant, "in all the excitement last night, I forgot to mention it, but did you hear that sound behind us when we first saw Thane Mortimer? It was the sound of some creature beating a hasty retreat, or I will eat my hat. Maybe that is the scent you smell?

"C'est possible, but I wonder about it all the same."

Tess of the Derby Villas stopped to scratch her ear, and she said, "The scent of *la* Princess is still lingering about here, so that at least is something. Confound her for a fool though. Out of all the bally scents wafting about in that dashed graveyard, what possessed her to land on the scent of dead roses? She must have smelt the yew trees, or the bones of the buried heroes, or even managed to mention she saw a few stone slabs here and there about the place. Any of that would have given us something better to go on when we wanted to figure out what kind of place she'd been in when taking her frolick. But oh no, all she had to report to us was that she'd sniffed a few dead roses. It's just the sort of exasperating vagary that gives princesses a bad name."

"Just so, *mam'zelle* Tess. Let us hope the last three scents are not so abstract, but now it is not of the princess I speak. I agree, she was here, it is certain, but also there is just now a new smell coming, do you not detect it yet?"

She raised her nose and sniffed the air studiedly. "But it can't be, not here. It's not possible."

"Eh, *normalement,* I might agree with you, it is not possible, but I would have said the same yesterday afternoon about the impossibility of spectral Danish Broholmers. By the sound of the stirring over there in the wood, I think we will soon have confirmation."

The famed detective spoke rightly, for in a few more minutes, a small, partly black head with a pointed nose emerged from the wood that lined the lane. A few more steps, and he revealed a furry form, crawling low to the ground and moving on all fours.

Tess of the Derby Villas would later say to her friend Prufrock, "No, Pruie, I could smell at once it was not a badger, and even if I had been suffering from the dickens of a cold, did you not hear me say about its bifurcated white stripe going head to tail? It was a skunk. That reality had to be faced up to at once, and its no good you giving me any guff about reality being an illusion. There are no modernists when it comes to being nose to nose with a skunk."

The skunk stared back at the two dogs, suspicion hinting about his eyes and tension increasing in his tail.

Tess of the Derby Villas said through her teeth in a low voice, "Say something reassuring to him, Potato. A skunk in a state of panic is the last thing we want."

Hercules Potato said, "Ah, *bonjour, monsieur le* Skunk. You are well today, I hope?"

The skunk did not appear ready to fire his ammunition just yet. He said, "*Salve.* Forgive me, but I must ask, I am sure you will understand why, I must ask who you are and what is your purpose in being so near my wood?"

"You make the conscientious enquiry, *monsieur le* Skunk. I am Hercules Potato, famed detective, and this is my bright and sporty assistant, *mam'zelle* Tess of the Derby Villas. We are near your wood because we are on a case. It is imperative we advance our investigation with due speed. We search for the scent of the chickens. If we might also know from you, by what name do you call yourself?"

The skunk, with the eyes of one who knows he must coldly and dispassionately assess all comers, inspected first one dog and then the other before he spoke. "My professional name is Mr. A. Hazardous Cabbage, H.M.E.P. Certified. However, my friends call me Haz, and you may do the same."

Tess of the Derby Villas said, "I for one am pleased as punch to meet you, Haz, truly I am. I was just saying to Potato here how I should jolly well fancy meeting a skunk as soon as can be hoped for. I hear you are, as a lot, the most smashing fun kind chappies, and I do hope you are equally pleased to meet us. We are two dashed delightful dogs, and I wish to stress, in no uncertain terms, there is not the slightest reason to be nervous of us." She wagged her tail with as much pep as she could give it, and let her pink tongue loll mildly from her mouth.

Hercules Potato hoped she was not laying it on too thick, but he approved her instinct to emphasize to a skunk there was not the least cause for being skittish. He said, "*Très bien*, here we all are, the two friendly dogs, and the one placid skunk. I notice, *monsieur* Haz, you introduced yourself with a set of credentials. What do they indicate, if I may ask you?"

"That is quite correct. I am an H.M.E.P. It designates me as one certified in hazmat materials management and in emergency preparedness."

"You don't say," said Tess of the Derby Villas, more than a little marvelled.

"How is it, *monsieur* Haz, that you come to be here in this country? It is not, I should have thought, the thing typical to find one of your number here, *n'est-ce pas?*"

"*Ita vero*, it is true what you observe. I am not a native of this country," answered Mr. A. Hazardous Cabbage, H.M.E.P. Certified. "I first came here *ab homine* factum. That is to say, by human deed. I believe I am not mistaken in thinking that these humans are what dogs such as yourselves refer to as heroes?"

"Ah, yes, the heroes, it is true," said Hercules Potato, "and I see that you are familiar with the Latin as well as well as with the hazmat management. You are truly an academic skunk, *monsieur* Haz and your heroes, they are fond of you?"

The skunk said, "As far as companions go, they were decent enough in the beginning, but as I grew, they became shy about having me in the house so often. The day came when it was decided it would be best for everyone if we parted ways and we said our valediction."

"Bally rotten," said Tess of the Derby Villas, "they chucked you out? I call it a dirty business. Not the stuff of heroes, to be sure. They must have been a sorry lot of what we dogs call antiheroes.

It's no end a pity you got mixed up with the likes of them. Blighters of their ilk do everyone a bad turn. So now you are in this wood on your own, eh? No cozy fires? No bits of bacon? It's pretty hard luck. I offer you my condolences."

"Thank you, I am sure, but it is not as bad as you make it out to be," said Haz. "We skunks do better in the wild than does your kind, *canis domesticis*. Unlike dogs, I am, I do assure you, quite comfortable and happy on my own."

Hercules Potato said, "*Magnifique*, if you are contended, *monsieur* Haz, all is well. Now if you please, might you tell to us if you have seen a dog near this wood a day or two ago? She is one of the white Borzoi, magnificent and impossible, but perhaps you saw her when she came through here a day or two ago?"

"Unfortunately, I cannot help you. I have been away on business. I am only just back this morning, so you will understand that is why I cannot speak to your question."

Tess of the Derby Villas later said to her friend Prufrock, "I dearly wanted to ask what sort of business calls a skunk away from his wood, but I didn't want to risk being offensive. I rather think it could be just as risky to offend a skunk as it is to make him nervous."

"I see," said Hercules Potato. "Well, perhaps you could tell us instead, if you know where we might find a nearby congress of chickens?"

"You will find them if you go through to the other side of this wood. I have no use for chickens myself, but I have seen the ones of which you speak. I can tell you, it is best to leave those particular chickens to themselves. They do not, you understand, welcome company with fondness."

"Thank you, it's jolly decent of you to give us the good old warning, Haz, but I think two dogs against any number of chickens are likely to come out on top," said Tess of the Derby Villas. "As much as we would love to continue this pleasant chat, we had better get a move on. We are in a race against the day as it were, so it doesn't do to stand about chatting. We shan't linger in your wood, and we'll be out of your fur as soon as we get to the other side."

Mr. A. Hazardous Cabbage, H.M.E.P. Certified, nodded his head curtly then said, "I must be careful, you understand, about any who come through my wood, but I am not unreasonable about it. I will leave you to your business. I wish you a good day. *Vade in pace.*"

With this benediction, he disappeared into the thicket, and the path through to the wood stood open for the two dogs to enter.

"Whew," exclaimed Tess of the Derby Villas, "happening on a skunk is deuced more agonising than happening on an old ghost dog any day, but we did manage to keep our Haz in a state of graceful calm. What's more, we know where to go to find the chickens. On the whole, I'd say we are doing well for our morning, Potato."

The wood did not prove to be a thick or interesting one, but Hercules Potato continued to notice the mysterious scent that had puzzled him yesterday all along the way. From the graveyard through this wood today, it persisted. Soon however, he had a different scent to register. Within a short time, they came out into the open air—an open air rife with the scent of the chickens.

"*Finalement,*" said Hercules Potato, "a scent that does not suffer from the vagueness."

The two dogs stood together assessing the dynamics of the scene before them. In the foreground, ran a fence. It bore an unmistakable hole, the obvious point of exit for the princess when she took leave of these chickens that had so rattled her.

Tess of the Derby Villas sniffed at it and said, "Hooray Henrietta left her odor here right enough."

In the background, about five hundred steps as the dog trots, they saw a gate opposite. Hercules Potato continued to sniff along the ground as his assistant said, "I don't suppose the gate on the other side just swung open and let her in. There must be a hole in the fence on that side too, or perhaps she just jumped over it. I say, those chickens are a rather posh lot."

Hercules Potato focused his eyes once more on the company of chickens and he agreed with his assistant. There were surprisingly pretty. Pecking about in the dirt, they composed a perfect picture of peace and tranquility, an embodiment of the quintessential dream of farm life. Taking in the scene stretched out before him, Hercules Potato said, "Ah yes, *mam'zelle* Tess, they are attractive, *n'est pas?* There was once the hero artist, a *monsieur* Frank Paton. He liked to paint the chickens in the so rich colours. I think he would have enjoyed an opportunity to paint these chickens."

"They do look like they could hold their own in the Most Beautiful Chicken pageant."

"The princess, she called these chickens the creatures wild and vicious, and the skunk too, he warned us they are not safe. It is curious, *non?*"

"I can't see even generally that a chicken could be a risk to a dog, and certainly not show ponies like these."

"*D'accord, mam'zelle* Tess. It will not be difficult to go across this farm, and we may also enjoy a luncheon delicious."

This prospect boosted their spirits, and they made ready to enter through the hole in the fence. It is, of course, folly of the first order for two dogs to imagine they can gain safe passage through a chicken farm. Later, Tess of the Derby Villas would tell her friend Prufrock, "I am sure I don't know what we could have been thinking. The moment we shuffled through the hole in the fence, the tranquil scene transformed into the charge of the light brigade."

"Look sharp, Potato," cried Tess of the Derby Villas, as fair two hundred chickens rounded towards them with raised wings and outraged beaks.

"Jappe, jappe, jappe" barked Hercules Potato, running as fast as he could against a rising tide of dust and a peep of hens flying into his face. "These chickens will end me with their clucking and their pecking and their feathers flying. Oh, *mam'zelle* Tess," he moaned above the din, "This must be the end." He began to lose speed and to be dragged down to the ground. "There will be no more of the famed detective," he gasped. "He will be only the detective dead, jappe, jappe."

Tess of the Derby Villas shunted a chicken to the side with the flick of her muzzle, as her rear flank filled with a chattering of churlish chicks nipping at her hindquarters.

"Grr-rah, grr-rah," she barked, springing to Hercules Potato's side, urging him onward. "They're just chickens, Potato. For the love of bacon, be a dog and pull yourself together. Grr-ah, grr-ah."

She grabbed hold of his collar between her teeth and dragged him through the battery of clucks and squawks and feathers and jabbing beaks. Their ears rang with the din of the battle all around them, but they began to gain on the gate little by little. Soon, they got out ahead of the furious hoard of hens. As they reached the gate, Tess of the Derby Villas shouted, "There's no hole. How will we get out?"

As she later told her friend Prufrock, "By Jove, Pruie, with the running start I had, I could have jumped over the bally thing, and it must have been the very thing the princess herself did. Potato, though, was in no condition to attempt the same feat, and it would hardly have been playing the game for me to leave a dog behind in a rum-do like that."

Hercules Potato, breathing heavily, looked back at the cloud of much roused poultry advancing on them. He shouted, "We must dig, *immédiatement.*"

"So," finished Tess of the Derby Villas to her friend Prufrock, "We raised high our bright tails and dug."

Quick as lightening, the two dogs set to clawing the ground with a fierce burst of energy, propelled to effectiveness by the yet-live peril behind them. Dirt flew up and pebbles catapulted out from behind their frantic hind legs, going straight into the eyes of several chickens charging at the fore of the advancing peep. Hercules Potato just felt the nip of a vicious beak as he and his bright and sporty assistant squeezed head first under the fence. They scrabbled up to the other side and felt as if they had entered a blessed and perfect land, safe at last from the onslaught of aggrieved chickens.

~

CHAPTER VI

THE DAY OF DISASTER

*H*ercules Potato and Tess of the Derby Villas kept on across fairly easy territory for the main part of the day. The scent of the Princess Anastazia seemed to be fading somewhat. They could still smell traces of her, but it was not the robust scent they followed out of Dale-on-Tweedy-Down the day before. The mysterious smell he first began to notice near the graveyard continued to crop up, and the question of what it was and what it's importance to the case might be, occupied a good deal of his thought as they went along.

As they approached a more heavily wooded area, they plopped down to rest onto a shady spot of soft grass. A drink of water and bite of food would not have gone amiss, but there was nothing on offer at present. Their empty stomachs rumbled in unison.

Hercules Potato said, "What idiots we were, *mam'zelle* Tess, to stumble through a farm full of the chickens most succulent, yet here we sit with the stomachs empty."

"Dash it all, Potato," she said. "You are forgetting it was the wrong moment to attempt sitting down for a quiet meal."

"*Peut-être,*" he said, "but still, we might have thought of grabbing a small bit of something for a take away, *non?*"

"Oh, do give over, Potato," she said, irritation rising in her voice. "All of this talk about eating is useless, and it makes everything worse." She pulled at the sack around her neck and wrestled it off. "And another thing, I don't see why I have to keep this blasted sack round my neck the whole way. Why can't you take a turn with it?" She gave it an emphatic kick in his direction.

"*Impossible,* the famed detective, he does not carry the sacks around the neck. Always, this is the job of his assistant."

"Oh is it?" said Tess of the Derby Villas, springing to all fours, "That makes you about as useless an old sod as our bugger all princess with her holy, 'we are far too vastly over-precious to talk to you' sort of attitude."

"And just where do you think you would you be right now without me? Without my nose and my analysis? Without my insistence on the scents and the logic, you would still be chasing your tail in a circle back by the brook in Dale-on-Tweedy-Down, never even knowing about a graveyard."

"At least I could jolly well have a sip of water," she retorted. "I don't see what use you are at this detective bit. For all your sniffing and thinking, we are nowhere with the Colonel's plan, and you strike me as incapable of getting us into a new plan with any sort of haste or chop-chop."

"The scents and the logic do not obey demands for hot haste and the chop-chop," he said, his offended ego incensed, "but always they reveal the answers with the work of time. You fast paced youth, you want only the solutions quick, *vite, vite. Mais non,* even if there is the hunger and the thirst, the slow work of the scents and the logic, it is the most reliable way to work a case."

"Stuff your scents and logic," said Tess of the Derby Villas, unmoved.

Hercules Potato's ears sprang to attention, but it was not on account of his irate assistant's grumbling. He had smelled the danger first, then, he heard it, ever so quiet in the grass. He slid an eyeball sideways and made a sight confirmation—an unnerving pair of eyes fixed upon him from a few paces away.

"*Mam'zelle* Tess," he whispered tensely, "do not move. There is a snake in the grass. Just over there. It is watching us, and I think it too has the luncheon on its mind."

Tess of the Derby Villas froze as advised, but she slid her eyes sideways in an effort to see the snake. "Is it moving?" she asked tersely.

"*Non, pas encore.* It is so far still. I think it waits for its best moment."

"Should we try and do a runner, do you think?" She asked nervously, adding, "I like action a lot more than I like waiting around for the worst to happen."

"*Non.* The snake, it would be too quick," he whispered. "It would catch one of us for sure. I can think only of one thing to do. I will make the movement false, and the snake will leap out to bite me. But you, *mam'zelle* Tess, you must make the movement quick. You must be faster than the snake. Spring forward and bite its neck before it reaches me. You can do that?"

"Yes, I rather think I can, but what if I miss it?"

"If you miss it, you must let it bite me, and you must run for your life."

Tess of the Derby Villas swallowed a lump in her throat. "Well, I'm not going to miss it," she said hoarsely.

Still in a low voice, he said, "*Bien*. The snake, it is so positioned that when it springs towards me, it will pass by you on your left side. Ready yourself to strike. I will move in the three counts."

"I am ready," she answered. "I'm crackling with nerves, but I won't let you down, Potato."

Hercules Potato began to count.

"Un." The breeze rustled through the tree leaves.

"Deux." A fly buzzed and landed on Tess of the Derby Villas' ear.

"Trois!"

Hercules Potato sprinted for the trees behind him. The snake shot out across the space of the field like an arrow sprung from a bow. Hissing rage, lest its prey escape, it sped intelligence of its location across the grass, and the success of either side hung in a vital half-second. In one moment, Hercules Potato turned his head and saw the snake flying towards him, its jaws open, its forked tongue leering out at him. In the next moment, he saw the snake, its neck broken, hanging limply from the mouth of Tess of the Derby Villas.

She tossed her head and flung the snake high across the grass, spitting and choking and shaking herself all over. This done, she said, "Nasty, vile tasting thing. I wouldn't eat it even if I knew I would never again find food in all the world."

"*Mam'zelle Tess*," said Hercules Potato, bowing his head to her, "you saved my life."

"Well there's no need to make a parade about it," she said. "Snakes are notorious for causing one mischief or another." She put her head once more through the strap of the contentious sack and urged the famed detective, "Let's just get out of here and find the next scent, Potato."

"Oui d'accord," agreed Hercules Potato. "On to the scent of the fish, and one may hope, to the luncheon." Together, they trotted into the wood. Behind them, the glittering sun shone down upon the dead snake, lying harmless in the verdant pasture.

As they moved through the quiet coolness beneath the tangled, leafy roof above them, neither dog spoke of the harrowing event they had just come through. They kept silent, and they kept their noses to the ground, seeking, finding and following the trail of the lost Princess Anastazia through the wood. Just as their pace began to lag from their wearying day, Hercules Potato urged, "We must try to go a little farther. Even in this wood, I sense that the day, it is finishing. It is troubling, *n'est-ce pas?* Every day as it passes by us, risks the loss of the two scents."

"Maybe not, Potato, maybe not. These seem to be the kind of scents that stay put. I think we can find the scent of fish, even if it should rain."

"True," he agreed, "and perhaps it is also true of the scent of the chocolate in its factory, but it is not so much those scents I worry about losing. It will be of dire trouble to us if we lose the scent of the princess to the rain. It is weak even now, but it is all we have to confirm to us that we are truly on the course correct. Also, I would not like for the rain to wash away the smell of the mysterious scent before I am able to identify what it is."

He put his nose forward and sniffed again. He said, "This mysterious scent, it is one I somehow think I have smelled before, *mais non*, it is at the same time elusively unfamiliar. I must discover what it means. It is important. Of that I am sure."

"All well and good, but do you smell any fish, Potato?"

The two dogs stopped. Hercules Potato sat and lifted his nose skyward. A gentle wind swept in from beyond the wood and carried with it a scent positively teeming with fish.

"Nous y allons," he shouted, and they tore down the woodland path hot upon the trail of the scent of the fish. Soon, they not only

smelled the fish, but they could hear the sound of a gently drifting river.

"It's dinner time," cried Tess of the Derby Villas. They did not have far to run. The wood ended at a towpath along a generous bank of lovely green grass. Soft, yellow sand spread down towards a river full of fish. The two dogs stopped and stared in amazement at the largess before them.

"A bridge would be a handy thing to have about now, Potato. Did la Princess mention one when you spoke with her?"

"*Non*, she made not the mention of it. She is maybe the strong swimmer and did not need the bridge. We however, are not so fortunate, and we will not get across this river without one."

"Speak for yourself, Potato. I've never been a dog to decline a brisk swim in a placid bit of water, and bridge or no, I'm starving."

Speeding to the water, she dove in and began to splash about, hoping to catch a few fish for the both of them. Hercules Potato approached the river with less enthusiasm. The current went gently by, though it was barely what one could call a current. He dipped in a front paw. He stared longingly at the fish he could see swimming about in slightly deeper water, but he did not think his short little legs would take him out to where they were. Then too, his weak, miniscule jaw would not be large enough or strong enough to catch a fish.

A Belgian Griffon of a past era would have had a snout and a jaw to competently deal with these fish, but that was a dog of yesteryear. Hercules Potato, a Belgian Griffon of the present day configuration, thought to himself what short work the highly esteemed Vizslas, Cassius and Epimone, would make of these fish.

He shook himself out, and this helped him to think along better lines. It may be he could not swim, and he could not snap up his own meal, but he could follow the scents and the logic, and this alone sufficed to boost his ego and make him puff out his chest. Then, he caught site of his reflection in the river's tranquil surface. Mud caked his fur, and little bits of sticks and brambles stuck to him at his ears and in his beard and moustache. His spat-like markings were not even visible beneath the layers of dirt and dust that covered them.

He tried dipping himself in the water, but as he had nothing to dry himself with, when he went back up to the grassy bank, the sand clung all over his wet fur. Still a mess, his stomach rumbled again. Fortunately, and despite not being a Vizsla herself, Tess of the Derby Villas had a splendid catch piled on the riverbank.

She came up out of the water and tossed a fish in his direction. "Tuck in, Potato. There's plenty more."

"You are most kind," he yelled back to her. He grabbed the fish in his mouth and settled down on the grass to enjoy it. Tess of the Derby Villas pulled herself back up out of the water and shook herself out vigorously. She scooped up a fish for herself and plopped down at his side. She dropped her fish between her two front paws and dug in. Scarcely has any dog ever enjoyed a fish more than did these two in that moment.

"*Mam'zelle* Tess," said Hercules Potato as he ate, "I am sorry I refused to help you to carry the sack containing the royal chew toy of the princess. I acted ungraciously towards you, and I hope you will be most kind and please to forgive me?"

"Of course, Potato," she responded magnanimously, "I forgive you."

"*Bien*, and please allow me to carry the sack during our journey tomorrow."

"Absolutely, it's all yours. I am sorry as well for my flash of temper and what I said about the scents and logic. I went a bit barmy I'm afraid. It was hunger and thirst making me tetchy."

Hercules Potato noticed his appearance had not been the only one to suffer from the rigors of their case. "*Mam'zelle* Tess," he said, "your once so jaunty red bow, I am sorry to see it is now in the tatters."

"Is it? I expect so. I wager mine lasted a good deal longer than did the one my namesake wore at the beginning of her story. I dare say my heroes will put it right when I get home."

"It is all the fault of this case most arduous, *n'est-ce pas*? If only it had been as the Colonel supposed, the mere work of one day."

"Well," said Tess of the Derby Villas drowsily, "if knights were baronets, we'd all be kings." She yawned and got up to stretch out her legs and find a pleasant spot on which to pass the night. She chose a tuft of velvety grass up a bit closer to the wood and neatly settled into it for a restoring night's sleep. Hercules Potato joined her, and also rested his head, but he felt the distraction of too much worry to fall to sleep. If they could have started out to search for the scent of the chocolates tonight, it would have been preferable.

Being too much worn out from their journey thus far, they could not continue without this rest. Dogs are handy at a sprint, he reflected, but they are not suited in the least to marathons. As he had feared at the outset, the long, swift legs of the Borzoi carried her farther and faster across a vast distance than they could go with their eight legs between them. He worried too because he smelled the distinctive scent of approaching rain flutter in to mix with the night air and the light breeze.

By the time the sun was near to midday tomorrow, he anticipated, dark clouds would amass in front of it, and a heavy rain would be the result. The Colonel's Four-Point-Plan had not been designed for a case that went on as long as this one. They would need to start off early tomorrow. With the rain coming, they must, if at all possible, stay ahead of it.

Would there be a bridge? Another major worry to settle, if it turned out, as he feared it must turn out, that the Princess came from the other side of the river. Still, now was not the time for the worries. With the stomach full and the thirst quenched, now was the time for the sleep restoring. He rested contentedly under the starry sky and slipped into sleep as the gentle warmth of the spring evening drifted around him, and the sound of water lapped softly back and forth, tenderly stroking the sand.

~

HERCULES POTATO AWOKE the next morning feeling extremely annoyed. Then he understood why. A sharp rock was poking its inflammatory edge into the fleshy underside of his belly. He shifted and felt a further moment's pang as he realised he was no longer nestled side by side with the Lady Stella, as he had just been dreaming. Resigning to wakefulness, he indulged himself in a stretch-out. He sniffed, and then he frowned.

Rain was most assuredly making its approach. If they met any luck at all today, they would reach the scent of the chocolate quite soon, and the Four Point Plan would be over before the rain arrived to wash away the remaining scents. Otherwise, they were at risk of being soaked and stranded on a case with no surviving scents to guide them to the palace of the princess.

As this disturbing thought struck him, he saw Tess of the Derby Villas busy at the work of collecting breakfast. She had kindly delivered him a fish to start in on. While he nibbled on it, he noted the sack containing the chew toy of the princess lay a safe distance away from the river's edge. Tess of the Derby Villas exited the water and indulged in a brisk shake out.

The famed detective called to her, "*Mam'zelle* Tess, I will be just the brief moment in the wood and then we must begin to hunt about for a bridge. We must hurry too, because the rain, it is coming."

"Rightio, Potato," she shouted back.

Hercules Potato nodded, then rose to all fours and went a few paces into the wood with the idea of finding a worthy tree to bless. He smelled again the mysterious scent, so familiar yet so unknown at the same time. What was it? He was running out of time. If only it would not rain too soon.

Tess of the Derby Villas sat down on the bank of the river to warm herself in a beam of morning sunlight. Though the river had been calm yesterday, it now rushed by with considerably more gusto. She muttered aloud to herself, "We will never get across the river while it's like that." Then she lifted her nose as a scent floated past it. She sniffed it and murmured, "But it can't be." Then, just as something streaked behind her, she turned her head quick as lightning, but she had turned too late.

His beneficence shared with a deserving tree, Hercules Potato began to sniff an unnerving smell. A cry of alarm rang out from the riverside, and he raced through the trees to answer the call of distress—more potato than god, tis only too true—but still, Hercules Potato raced to the scene.

He shot out of the wood and sped towards the river, now rushing in furious torrents down stream. Tess of the Derby Villas was precariously balanced on a protruding rock in the middle of it, clutching the chew toy of the Princess Anastazia between her teeth. There was no time to spare in wondering what had happened. Hercules Potato paced anxiously up and down along the river's edge trying to think of some way to rescue his stranded assistant.

An idea flashed into his mind. A branch, he must find a sturdy and long tree branch to send out to her to cling to. He looked frantically back at the wood, and there, sitting cool as she pleased, her tail gliding to and fro, sat the very shady Tabby cat, MissTree. It had in fact been her scent that he had smelled in the wood only a moment ago. Without stopping to consider why it was that she had happened upon them, he called as he rushed towards her, "Quick, *mam'zelle* MissTree, help me to find a branch to help *mam'zelle* Tess."

"It's too late for that now, Potato," she answered smoothly, as Hercules Potato turned in time to see a swift surge of water swell from upstream. In an instant, Tess of the Derby Villas was gone.

"*Mam'zelle* Tess," he cried, running back down along the river back, hoping in vain to spot her coming back up to the surface. He stopped and looked expectantly across to the opposite bank, but she had not come out anywhere that he could see.

"She is gone," said the malevolent voice coming up beside him. "No mo-rrr-e assistant, no mo-rrr-e chew toy. You-rrr case is in ruins, isn't it now?"

Hercules Potato turned to the cat and said, "So, it is you, *mam'zelle* MissTree, you have been following us, careful, I suppose, to stay far enough away to prevent our smelling your presence? You have come a long way to meddle, and I ask myself why?"

"Why? It is as I told you before, because I enjoy seeing you make a fool of yourself. It makes me happy."

Hercules sniffed her studiedly, and then he asked, "And you are happy now? This tragedy, it makes you the happy cat?"

"Assu-rrr-edly it does. It was not my plan to have your assistant drown, but these things happen, don't they now? What is the loss of one mo-rrr-e dog, when I myself am so happy to see your case in ruins?"

"I may have been powerless to save, *mam'zelle* Tess, but I am not powerless to solve this case, I assure you, *mam'zelle* MissTree. If I do not solve it, her death will have been in vain, and I will not allow it."

"Her death is in vain, and you can help nothing, Potato. You are lost now. The princess splashed across easily enough a few days ago, but you cannot swim, can you now? You have no more royal chew toy, and you have no more assistant. Go back to Dale-on-Tweedy-Down and face your failu-rrr-e."

"*Non,* even if all is grim, Hercules Potato, he does not give up his case before it is solved, *jamais.*"

"I myself will go back to your precious Dale-on-Tweedy-Down and tell them all your case has come to nothing and you are lost with it. What can you do if you stay here? Drown in the river too? Why don't you, two less dogs in the world will make a further happiness for me."

MissTree turned and glided back up the riverbank, then disappeared into the wood. While the river rushed on beside him, the famed detective turned from the very shady Tabby cat in disgust, and began to determinedly trot downstream. After all, he might yet find Tess of the Derby Villas scrambling up the bank farther down. The truth, though, was that he had spoken more confidently to MissTree than he actually felt. What could he do now, alone, with no bridge, and with the rain fast approaching? The bright and sporty Tess of the Derby Villas might indeed be drowned, and he began to sink into hopelessness.

He stopped and hung his head down, feeling the weight of his sorrow becoming too much for him to master. Then the words of the Colonel floated back to him, "Hope is certainly something a rescue dog knows a lot about."

Could hope still do something for Tess of the Derby Villas? He did not know, but he remembered the princess, still separated from her hero, and found better courage. He had not been able to save his assistant, but he said aloud to the angry river, "While I am still the famed detective, I will not give up the case until the Princess Anastazia and her true hero, they are restored to one another."

He continued to trot down stream, determined that Tess of the Derby Villas would not have drowned in vain. His mind went back to ancient Greece, where once a beautiful hero's life had ended in tragedy. Finding their beloved Iphigenia dead, a chorus of sad hero voices had poured out their grief with song, singing to the heavens in lamentation, 'And like her song be thine, sorrow, sing sorrow: but good prevail, prevail."

CHAPTER VII

THE SURPRISE ATTENDANT WITH THE
SCENT OF THE CHOCOLATE

*H*ercules Potato continued a course down stream along the river. He did not know at which point along it the Princess had splashed her crossing, but at least he was going in the direction the river had taken Tess of the Derby Villas. He pulled up abruptly when he noticed the scent of the Princess

Anastazia mingled in the grass he now trod upon. He sniffed and reflected. It was faint, but it clearly indicated that she had come from this far down stream after all.

To be once again on the trail of a relevant scent was uplifting. Every now and again, he sought for signs that Tess of the Derby Villas might have found her way out of the river, but in this hope, he continued to meet disappointment.

Here and there, he felt drops of rain upon his fur, and he knew he would soon lose the scent of the princess altogether. Her fading scent continued leading him downstream along the river, until it brought him around a significant bend. When this flattened out, he saw it. As a sailor after weeks adrift at sea might cry out, "Land ho," so Hercules Potato cried out, "Bridge ho."

Its perfect solidity arched gracefully above the fast moving river — a vision of delivery rising up to rescue a trapped dog. How like that magnificent but impossible Borzoi to leave such a monumentally important detail out of her story. If he had known for certain that she came over a bridge instead of splashing across the river, they would not have lingered where they did last night. Then he wondered if MissTree merely guessed that there was no bridge?

When he reached it, he sniffed and found confirmation that the princess had indeed crossed over on it. He sniffed also for any scent to tell him if *mam'zelle* Tess had also found the bridge, but in this he once again met disappointment. He could not detect a trace of her here. However, he did again detect the mysterious scent that had puzzled him all along the case. It now puzzled him no more. He understood what it signified even if he could not yet explain why it should be so.

After crossing the bridge, the famed detective paused to survey the lay of the land in front of him. It was all open fields far and wide. In the middle ground, he spotted a flock of sheep, grazing with the attitude of the habitually unconcerned. In the foreground, a new complication met his nose and eyes. Though the tract of land appeared on its surface to be unpopulated by current activity, he sniffed the recent deviance of moles. It did not take long for him to spot their signature holes blemishing the ground in all directions.

Moles had most definitely been at work here. Just as he had warned the Colonel, their underground subterfuge went on in even the most wholesome of places. He trotted further into the territory, sniffing the ground here, testing the air there, but the moles had churned the earth too much. They had disordered any scents that once rested on the surface. The scent of the princess went cold. To add further complication to his search, a fat raindrop plopped down on the famed detective's nose.

He had always heard it was useless to attempt any conversation with sheep, but as these sheep were his only possible witnesses, he decided to try his paw at making an enquiry of one them. He risked enough optimism to entertain the possibility that, perhaps, these sheep might be of a brighter nature than is generally reputed to their species.

Hercules Potato, Belgian Griffon and famed detective had erred when he expected to find safe passage through a chicken farm. In expecting to speak with a bright sheep, he erred again. To do him credit though, he could not possibly have known he was striding up to take a sophist sheep into conversation. He approached a fluffy, white sheep, who stood with a vague expression on his face, chewing a staggering mouthful of grass. His fellow congregation spread out nearby, doing much the same thing in much the same vague way.

Hercules Potato cleared his throat and began politely, "*Bonjour, monsieur le* Sheep. I see you enjoy the luncheon most fine, so I will not trouble you for long, but I am searching for the scent of a lost dog, and it is made difficult by the scent of the many moles rummaging under the ground."

Here, he paused, as the sheep swallowed his mouthful of grass. Seeing that sheep did not yet intend to give voice, the famed detective continued to his questions. "If you please, I wonder two things. Can you tell to me where I might find the scent of the chocolates, and also, have you seen a large, white dog come through here in the last few days?"

To his horror, the sheep let loose a horrendous burp, and without begging to be excused, he asked absently, "Large and white wot?"

"Dog," said Hercules Potato through gritted teeth.

"You don't need to look too far to see large and white seems to me," laughed the sheep as he indicated his sistren and brethren dotting the pasture, "but yer lookin for chocolate moles you say?"

Hercules Potato pursed his lips, but he answered patiently, "*Non, monsieur* le Sheep, I am looking for the scent of the chocolate—that much is true—but as for the moles, *non*. I wish to avoid them. I am looking for—"

"Are you a mole?" asked the sheep.

If Hercules Potato had ever been insulted by comparisons with teacup poodles, he forgot it now. "*C'est absurde, non. Non*, of course I am not a mole," he sputtered. Regaining his composure, he said with dignified calm, "*Je suis chien*. I am no such thing as a mole."

"Yer quite wrong there," retorted the sheep. "There be such things as moles. I saw one just a minute ago. I've not seen a dog a-for, though. It's dogs as maybe don't exist."

The miniscule jaw of Hercules Potato fell open, and for a moment, he was stunned into silence. He saw clearly he must begin again. "*Monsieur le* Sheep, you must have seen a dog before. I say nothing of the dog who stands before you now, but you must know all about the sheep dog, *n'est-ce pas*? Of that I am sure."

"I can't rightly say as I have. We don't have dogs round our parts. Now, what we do have oft times round here is him what's called Sergeant Peppy."

"Sergeant Peppy?"

"Yes, that's right, as I said, though he's none too popular with us sheep. Comes round a lot more then he's welcome too, he does, and always barky and bossy he is too, very sure of himself he is. Says there be such things as right and wrong he does."

Hercules Potato attempted to say something towards steering conversation back to the scent of the chocolate, but *monsieur le* Sheep was just beginning to warm to his theme and he would not be interrupted. "I've tried to tell him once if I've tried to tell him a hundred times. Right and wrong is nothin to a sheep. There's naught but what we do and what we don't do. 'Course he's barky and won't stand down. Not one is he to accept there's nothin that's safe to be sure about. Mind you though, he's not a dog. He's been called an Australian Shepard in my hearin, but I don't put much stock in definitions as like. Are you sure you ain't no mole then?"

Hercules Potato chewed on his lip. Even Pookie Shams, never what one could call frantic with brains at the best of times, might have easily run away with the prize in an intellectual match against this committedly sophist sheep. He gave it one more go, and said, "I am a dog, I assure you, *monsieur le* Sheep. You might also be interested to learn this Australian Shepherd you speak of is a dog as well. We are both the dogs."

"I don't know 'bout that. If you're to be believed, and Sergeant Peppy is a dog, he has enough of a size to him. Not like you. You seem to be about the size of a mole to me, but you say you ain't no mole? Are you cousin to a mole then?"

The pride of Hercules Potato had never before received such a volley of devastating blows. He insisted again, "I am nothing to do with the moles, *monsieur le* Sheep. I am not a mole, nor am I a cousin to a mole. I have no association with moles in any way."

"Not even a first cousin once removed?"

"*Non. Je suis chien.* A dog, a Belgian Griffon to be precise."

At last, a light seemed to flicker in the sheep's eyes, and he said, "Yer a Belgie then are you? Like one of them chocolates? My missus does go on about them Belgian chocolates, loves 'em she does. So that's what you are, a chocolate?"

This left Hercules Potato to ask himself, oh death, where is thy sting? He thought just then of the post-modernist author hero, Mr. Samuel Beckett, and his story about strange heroes who sat in rubbish bins and spoke nonsense to each other. Mr. Beckett might have been a hero who could find common philosophy enough to work with this sophist sheep, but the famed detective could not do it. He said, "*Non, non, monsieur le* Sheep, I am not a chocolate, but as I said, I search for the scent of the chocolates."

"Well now, there you go again. I do wish you would get your story straight, mister. I heard you say afore that yer out for them moles as do dig about underground."

Hercules Potato could endure no more.

"I think," he said in a faltering voice, "I must make no more trespass upon your time. *Bonne Journée, monsieur le* Sheep."

"And a good day to you too, mister, but there is just one more thing you might consider afore you go."

Anticipating some fresh insult, Hercules Potato stoically resigned himself to his fate. "And what it is that, *monsieur le* Sheep?"

"That is, if its dogs yer lookin for, might I suggest you try sailin to the end of the world?"

"To the end of the world?"

"There's lots of mighty strange things do go on at the end of the world, or so I hear tell. If yer goin a find dogs anywhere, to my mind, it would have to be there."

Hercules Potato could find no words to answer this suggestion, and taking his leave of the sophist sheep, he wandered away in a bewildered stupor. As he tottered off, a daftly jovial sheep went docilely over to *monsieur le* Sheep and asked him, "Who was that you were just talking to, Mr. Threepsheep?"

"Well, I can't rightly say, Mrs. Threepsheep. Poor fella, never properly introduced himself, he didn't. Mind you, to my way of thinkin, it's never possible to make anything out all the way, but I did put a few things together about him. He is a confused little chocolate, who lost a mole that he does not wish be acknowledged as his cousin."

Mrs. Threepsheep nodded appreciatively, and said to her husband, "He sounds dear as ducks he does, Mr. Threepsheep."

"Ducks, Mrs. Threepsheep, is the one thing as never entered into the conversation."

~

AN AGGRIEVED CHICKEN IS, of course, a matter altogether different in nature from a sophist sheep. Nonetheless, the effect of an encounter with either is to be left feeling fatigued in body and mind. As he could smell nothing of the princess, Hercules Potato lay down to rest and to clear his mind.

The logic reasserted its influence as the words of *monsieur le* Sheep, talking about his missus eating Belgian chocolate, floated back to him. Did sheep, put out in the middle of a pasture, routinely encounter chocolate of any description? He thought not. Not, unless, there was a chocolate factory nearby to keep them in a steady supply of it.

He stood up. Supposing pieces of chocolate often got dropped on the ground as factory heroes carried it home from the factory? He must indeed be close. He began sniffing about, and soon, he found an empty chocolate wrapper. It was not, strictly speaking, Belgian chocolate, for that must be made in Belgium. However, Hercules Potato could smell enough to allow it was at least chocolate made after the Belgian style. These distinctions would quiet naturally be lost on a sophist sheep, but no matter.

His continued investigation produced yet another empty wrapper, then another. As raindrops pelted his fur, he saw on the horizon a high, puffing column of white smoke set against the dark of the rain clouds. A steady stream of rain began to pour down on him, but Hercules Potato felt only the heat of being hot on the trail of the scent of the chocolates.

He hurried his pace in the direction of the white smoke, getting wetter and wetter all along the way. He paused at a street, across which a gated drive presented itself to his view. Behind this, he could see the bulk of a factory, but it was the bright red and pink box of "Belgian Style" chocolates emblazoning the front gate that gave him the most excitement.

He ran across the street shouting, "*Mam'zelle* Tess, we are here. We have found the scent of the chocolates."

Then he remembered and felt instantly deflated. He sat down in front of the gate and lowered his head, soaking wet beneath the torrent of rain. He remembered that Tess of the Derby Villas must now be lying in her watery grave, and there came to him the words of the hero poet, Lord Tennyson. "It was the closing of the day/She loos'd the chain, and down she lay/The broad stream bore her far away."

Hercules Potato shook his fur out vigorously, though it did him not the least bit of good. He thought to himself that he must put away for now the thoughts melancholy and tragic and think only of the case and of the scents and of the logic.

An imposing row of vertical iron bars formed the closed gate. It was not an obstacle for him, of course. His small dog's frame slipped effortlessly between the bars. The short drive ended in a parking area scattered with resting motorcars. The scent of the chocolate permeated through the rain as Hercules Potato sought shelter.

He made for an overhang of the building and found relief from the downpour. He again shook himself out vigorously and this time, beneath the overhang of the roof, it did do him some bit of good. A dry towel would have done him a great deal better, but he knew it was too much to hope for.

Here he would wait here for the rain to stop, but then to do what? His nails clicked nervously on the pavement, and the tags on his collar clinked together as he paced back and forth, thinking about what he should do next. The rain continued to stream down, but the overhang above him protected him from a further soaking.

He vaguely heard a dog bark in the distance beyond the factory. So absorbed was he in working out what to do next, he barely registered it in his mind. Here he was, at the last scent, the scent of the chocolates, but the rain would have washed away all remaining scent of the princess that could have led him back to her palace. What then, should be his next move?

While musing upon the utter collapse of the Colonel's Four-Point Plan, he heard more barking. This time, he paused his thoughts and his ears gave focused attention to the sound. Amidst the torrent of rain, a magnificent surprise burst in on him like a dark night suddenly lit up with fireworks. The bark was the unmistakable bright and sporty bark of the dog infused with all of the vim and zeal of youth.

Finally, he saw her, Tess of the Derby Villas, racing towards him from a clump of trees across the way. She took a flying jump over a picnic table and skidded to a stop at the front paws of Hercules Potato's stupefied figure.

"What ho, Potato," she said.

"*Mam* . . . *mam'zelle* - - T-T-T-ess?" he stuttered in disbelief.

"All present and correct," she said, and licked him on the ear.

"But . . . I . . . I saw you drown," he stammered, "and now here you are as if you . . . as, well, not at all like the blue spectral orb of Thane Mortimer."

"Don't be daft, Potato. I'm not a ghost. I am as alive as you are and just as nearly wet through too. You are looking a bit the worse for the wear, if you don't mind my saying so."

"Ah, and *mam'zelle* Tess, your red bow, it is missing completely now. It is a pity, but please to tell me, how is this oh-so-happy thing of seeing you alive possible?"

"Zounds, Potato," she answered, sitting down on her haunches. "I thought I was cheese toast too at first. Not only that, but it was dirty work at the crossroads."

"*Quoi?* The dirty work, how so? Please, *mam'zelle* Tess, tell to me all."

"Rightio, Potato. It was like this. When you went into the wood, I finished up my breakfast fish and sat down to watch the river. I was thinking I could still have made a go at crossing it, but with you not being able to swim, what could we do without a bridge? Then, a smell I knew all to well hit my nose at the same moment I felt a swift breeze of motion to the back of me. I turned my head and who do you think I saw?"

"Most probably, you saw the cat, MissTree."

"Quite correct, and that blast and wretch cat was there to make a sneak attack on the royal chew toy."

Hercules Potato took in a sharp breath. "Do you mean to tell to me that MissTree, she was not there only to watch, but to deliberately sabotage us?"

"Bang on the spot, Potato. False feline that she is, she had the princess' chew toy out of the sack and into her mouth in a flash. Then, with a wanton toss of her head, she flung it into the river."

"*Non*," gasped Hercules Potato.

"*Oui*," said Tess of the Derby Villas. "I cried out and dove in after it, and by Jove, I got my teeth into it too. That is just when you saw me caught up on the rock. I could tell you were desperate to help me, but what could you have done for dog in a fix like I was in just then? Not much, I expect."

"I thought if I found a long branch, it could help you, but there wasn't time, in the end, to find one."

"Jolly good of you to try, I am sure, but I am nothing if I am not a damsel in determination. I vowed long ago that no blast and wretch cat would ever be the end of me. As I clung to the rock, I saw her there on the bank, sitting prim as you please, her tail twining behind her, pleased as poisoned punch. It was the last thing I saw before the river rushed me from the stage, but I determined upon survival."

"*Mam'zelle* Tess, this is an account most astonishing. *Donc*, it was *mam'zelle* MissTree then, who was the cause of your near death? It is worse than I thought. She sabotaged the royal chew toy and almost lost for you your life? *C'est incroyable*."

"Feline and felony go together like birds of a feather."

Getting up to pace back and forth, the famed detective began to think aloud. "This cat, MissTree, she says it makes her happy to watch us fail to find the hero of the princess, but again, I ask myself, is it more than that? She is actively working against us. *Pourquoi*? Is it only because it makes her happy to do it? Ah, but no matter that for now, *mam'zelle* Tess, please to continue, how did you survive the river?"

The rain began to slacken as she resumed her tale of survival. "Well, I kept my head above the water as much as I could, but tried not to waste my energy fighting the current. I just let it take me along. I almost lost the royal chew toy, though. It slipped out of my mouth and got way out ahead of me, but my luck held, because it got caught in between a rock and some tree branches sticking out of the water. The current took me right by it. I grabbed hold of it once more, just going under a bridge."

Hercules Potato focused on her intently as he said, "What is this you say about the chew toy of the princess? Do I understand you correctly? Do you mean to tell me that you possess it still?"

"Oh yes, of course, I do." She indicated the spot with her muzzle as she said, "I left it right over there under those trees."

"*Magnifique*, proclaimed Hercules Potato, "although, it cannot do us much good if we cannot find the palace, but please, return to your story."

"As I was saying, the river swept me along beneath the bridge over troubled waters. You found it, I suppose? I hoped you would."

"*Oui, mam'zelle* Tess. I found it, *merci*. I also found a sophist sheep who does not believe that dogs exist."

Tess of the Derby Villas looked at him blankly. "He doesn't what?"

Hercules Potato waived her off. "Never mind," he said. "It was the interlude most wearying, but please to continue with what happened next?"

"Past the bridge, the river narrowed, and I found my moment to paddle back towards the bank. I came a long way down river in a hurry. Faster than trotting, I can tell you. I could see the chocolate factory from where I regained the ground. I sought shelter under those thick trees over there and sat down to wait for you to show up. It took you an age, by the way. What kept you?"

Hercules Potato said, "The subterfuge of the moles and the absurdities of the sophist sheep, they are almost enough to make the work of the scents and the logic grind to a halt, but not quite. They managed to bring me, in the end, to this last scent in the Colonel's Four-Point-Plan. Now we have the joy to be reunited here, there is still the work final to do before the case is solved."

~

CHAPTER VIII

THE IDEOLOGUE AT THE GATE

*T*he rain having trickled down to almost nothing, Tess of the Derby Villas said, "We can be clearing off from here soon, but what do the old scents and logic have to say about where we point our noses, now there is nothing left to smell?"

Hercules Potato drummed his nails on the concrete while he

considered her question. At length he said, "It is by no means an easy question to answer, *mam'zelle* Tess. To review, we have completed the Colonel's Four Point Plan. We have no more points to follow, and this rain has washed away all scent of the Princess Anastazia that might have led us easily to her palace. The scents, they can give us no more help at present."

Tess of the Derby Villas offered, "Maybe not. Now the rain has stopped, we might try searching for the scent of the palace. What does a palace smell like, do you suppose?"

Hercules Potato frowned. "Even assuming it is in fact a palace as the princess says it is, I do not think it would smell distinctively enough to search it out by the nose."

His companion waited expectantly while he sat lost in thought. "Well," she prompted him, "what do we do now?"

"As I see it, it must be the logic upon which we rely *en ce moment*, but my thoughts right now, they are all in pools." He took a few paces forward and sniffed the air. "The rain, it is over. I must sit and think. The scents, they are no more, but perhaps the logic, it will still be enough."

"Right," she said, "I'll leave you to it then. I saw a ramp earlier that warrants some investigation, so I'll just go and have a shufty while you sit and think."

She went round to the back of the building and scurried up the ramp that led into the warehouse. Noises and voices came from rooms deeper into the building, but there were no heroes to be seen in this room. She walked up, down, and across rows and rows of boxes stacked in towering piles. Her nose, of course, could tell her these boxes were filled to brimming with chocolates. She said to them as she went by, "Do stop taunting me so. I know dogs mustn't eat chocolate. You don't need to rub it in."

She began to sniff around for other less controversial nibbles and bitables. She came to a little area near the ramp entrance where some enterprising hero had set up a makeshift kind of kitchenette. There was no sink, but a refrigerator hummed in the corner. A few chairs surrounded a rectangular table. Several neatly laid out brown paper sacks rested on top of the table.

"Ah ha," she said aloud, "That's more the sight a dog wants to see at a time like this." She cast a glance behind her—still no heroes in sight. She leapt onto a chair, mounted the table top, seized two brown paper sacks between her teeth, then bolted with the speed of Mercury back down to the floor and out onto the ramp.

Emerging out of deep and ponderous thought, Hercules Potato saw his bright and sporty assistant charging towards him, two brown paper sacks flapping between her jaws.

"*Mam'zelle* Tess, I now know what to do."

She dropped the sacks down in front of him, panting and gasping for breath as she said, "I found a spot of lunch for us, Potato."

"What would I do without you, *mam'zelle* Tess?"

"Starve, I expect."

They tore into the sacks and out spilled an apple, a banana, one ham sandwich, one turkey sandwich, several biscuits, and a plum. Within seconds, only a shredded banana peel and a plum pit remained in evidence.

"Ah, *mam'zelle* Tess, now, we can get on with things," said a satisfied Hercules Potato. "As I was saying before you appeared with our luncheon, I now know what to do. *Vraiment*, it is the thing quite simple. I must be the idiot complete for not thinking of it before, but it was hard to think with clarity when the fur, it was wet and the stomach, it was empty."

"I do feel slightly pinched by remorse," broke in Tess of the Derby Villas. "Two factory heroes are not going to have their luncheon today."

"*Alors*, let them eat chocolate," said Hercules Potato. "As I was saying, we must find next the path the Princess Anastazia took as she chased after the scent of the chocolates and reached this factory. At the end of this path, more information may await us, or it may not. All we can do is to find out where it goes."

"Rightio, Potato, where is it I wonder?"

"*Donc*, we know we must not go out by the way of the front gate. Her path there would lead us back to the fish, not to the palace; that is quite clear. The gates, they must have been open on the day in question in order to let the lorries pass through them, else she could not have gone out that way herself. So, it is quite logical to deduce we must search on the back end of this chocolate factory for a path through the trees."

Tess of the Derby Villas nodded her head in agreement and said, "Nothing else for it then. Let's hop to sharpish."

"*Attends, mam'zelle* Tess, but where is the royal chew toy of the princess?"

"Oh, right, I'll just run and fetch it. I'll be back in a tick."

She was off in a flash and back in half the time. As she placed the chew toy at Hercules Potato's front paws, he said, "*Très bien, mam'zelle* Tess, it is because of you that we still have this proof so important to our case. You did well to keep ahold of it. *Alors*, we have now the path to find."

Tess of the Derby Villas once again scooped up the royal chew toy, and the two dogs took off at due speed towards the rear of the factory. A fairly thick grouping of trees met them there, and a path through them was not obvious. They lost some time running up and down along the wood's edge, finding no opening into the wood at all.

"It is strange, *mam'zelle* Tess, right here, I can smell the air is more free, as though it comes from along a path, but where is it?"

Tess of the Derby Villas sniffed at a pile of branches, and said, "I think it is here, but the rain and wind blew these loose branches around and now they are blocking the entrance."

They pawed together at the loose debris, and it cleared away without much resistance. This done, the path stood open before them. The famed detective said, *"Donc, mam'zelle* Tess, let us get the chew toy of the princess and be off down this path."

Tess of the Derby Villas, who had dropped the chew toy while she helped search for the path, retrieved it and stood ready with it between her teeth.

Hercules Potato said, "Ah, I forget we have no more the sack," and feeling magnanimous, he offered, "Please, *mam'zelle* Tess, allow me to have a turn to carry this burden most annoying."

"That's quite sporting of you, Potato," she said after she put the princess's chew toy at his forepaws. "I could do with a bit of a break from it, truth be told."

They ought to have got down the path in no time at all. Indeed, Tess of the Derby Villas got to the end of it within five minutes of starting down it, but Hercules Potato could not match her time. Returning back down the path, she discovered him locked in a fight with some brambles that had ensnared the princess' chew toy. As its size overwhelmed the Belgian Griffon's tiny mouth and scant jaw, he had resorted to dragging it along by one of its dangling threads. This then, resulted in the brambles getting hold of it.

Not for the first time in his life did Hercules Potato deeply lament the lost, strong and pronounced jaws of his rat catching ancestors. With much regret, he thought of those Belgian Griffons who won their fame catching rats in the horse stables. They would not have struggled to carry a mere chew toy as this. At least, he consoled himself, the Lady Stella was not present to see the bitter spectacle.

"You know, Potato," said Tess of the Derby Villas, "I think I might just bring the thing on myself. I rather expect we shall need your talents to be undistracted from here on out."

Hercules Potato sniffed nonchalantly and said, "Very well, *mam'zelle* Tess. If you insist, I will surrender the chew toy into your most able charge."

This time, they arrived at the end of the path together. A pavement crossed in front of them, and across the lane, they saw a welcoming stretch of houses neatly lined up side by side. Some were hedged in with shrubbery, others by low, stonewalls, and a few were trimmed with picket fences. As homes, they were perfectly charming, but the two dogs agreed between themselves that none could possibly answer to the description of a palace.

Up the lane and down the lane, intersections crossed in intervals, and choice of direction overwhelmed their decision-making. Tess of the Derby Villas let the royal chew toy fall to the ground as Hercules Potato said, "So many directions to choose from, *mam'zelle* Tess. All the scents, all the smells, they are washed away, and we are left to stab at innumerable guesses. It is the fine kettle of pickles, as they say."

"Fish," said Tess of the Derby Villas.

"Fish?"

"Yes, it's 'fish' you mean, 'A fine kettle of fish.' You can use pickle though, if you like. You can say 'we are in a pickle.' Either phrase works a treat to describe our scenario."

A few heroes passed by the two dogs as they stood at the opening of the path. These were the first heroes they had seen in days, and both dogs felt cheered at the smell of them. Hercules Potato gave them a friendly "Jappe, jappe, jappe," while Tess of the Derby Villas contributed her "grr-rah, grr-rah, grr-rah."

The heroes acknowledged them with smiles and "Good dogs," or "Hello there, pups," as they passed on about their business. However, one lovely little petite hero stooped down to have a better conversation. "Hello, doggies," she said, patting each on the head in turn, and giving Tess of the Derby Villas a pleasing scratch behind her ears. "You aren't lost I hope." Looking down at the royal chew toy, she said, "You look out now, or you might loose your toy. Here, let me help you."

To the great delight of Tess of the Derby Villas, the petite hero picked up the royal chew toy, and splitting its long threads of yarn into two sections, she tied it securely around her collar, right in the place where her red bow had once been attached. "There now," said the petite hero, "wherever it is that you are going, you won't loose your toy."

"Polly, what are you doing?" called a grand hero from up the pavement. "Do leave those dogs alone and catch up. We are frightfully late as it is."

"Must go to my piano lesson," whispered the petite hero, giving Tess of the Derby Villas one more scratch behind her ear before running to catch up her mother.

"I say, Potato, but that was bally good luck we just had. What a kind soul the petite hero Polly is. I wish I could have thanked her properly."

"*C'est vrai*, she is the kind soul, but it is the pity that she could not have told to us where to find the palace, *n'est-ce pas?*"

"Can't have everything, Potato. Maybe he can tell us over there."

Hercules Potato followed her gaze across the lane, to where a dog stood in one of the front gardens. He had seen them as well, and he barked out a sharp hark-who-goes-there?

"*Bien sûr*, a fellow dog. It is perfect," said Hercules Potato. "We need only the helpful witness in order to know where to go next."

Both dogs bounded across the lane, feeling boosted to no small degree. They approached the gate, and in between the spaces of its pickets, they could see a dog standing sentry at his post. Later, Tess of the Derby Villas would tell her friend Prufrock, "You might not think a yellow Labrador wearing pink and grey bunny ears can look officious, but this one could."

"That's as far as you go without identifying yourselves," said the Labrador, as Tess of the Derby Villas sniffed at the gate.

"*Bonjour, monsieur*, I am Hercules Potato, famed detective. You have heard of me before, *n'est-ce pas?*"

"Of course not. I know my duty, which is to stand at my watch and make sure no one comes through this gate. As far as you saying you are a detective, it sounds to me like you are part of a shifty lot. Detectives are snooping sorts, exactly the type of dogs who would love nothing better than to go slinking through a prohibited gate at the first opportunity."

Hercules Potato stared at him. Thus far on this case, he had been disgracefully treated by a vast company of aggrieved chickens, survived a snake's attempt to turn him into a light luncheon, been mistaken for a mole, and now he was likened to one who slinks. He rallied, however, and mastering his offended pride, which was learning to take the hits that came its way, he said with all politeness, "I do assure you, *monsieur*, Hercules Potato, he is not the slinker. My assistant and I — ah, if I may introduce her to you, this is *mam'zelle* Tess of the Derby Villas. To continue, we come to you in good faith, without the slinking. We are on a case most important."

"It's nothing to me whether you come on a case or in a box, but you are not going to come through this gate," declared the Labrador.

Tess of the Derby Villas attempted to lighten the tone, saying, "I say, old chap, what's with the fancy dress?"

The Labrador in bunny ears regarded her suspiciously and said, "If you think you can distract me with conversation about my attire while your friend here slips past this gate, well young miss, you can just think again."

"Look here," she said, "we don't give a flying fig for your revolting gate, but what I want to know is, what is the meaning of those Thumper's ears you've got on your head?"

The Labrador answered stiffly, "How my heroes take a fancy to dress me is not something I typically consider bears explaining to strangers."

Hercules Potato saw a chance to restore better feelings to the conversation and he said, "Ah, your heroes. They are the good heroes, *n'est-ce pas?*"

"They are indeed. I only came to them a short while ago, but they are more wonderful than I can describe. I look after them as seriously as any dog does who knows his duty."

"So I believe. You are a dog most conscientious. *S'il vous plait, monsieur* . . . ah, what, may I inquire, do you call yourself?"

A breeze fluttered in and began to play about with the pink and grey bunny ears as the Labrador answered, "My name is Ethelred. You may have heard of my ancient namesake, but don't let it give you any wrong impressions. I am ready, I assure you, to see you do not come through this gate."

"As you may recall my mentioning before," said in Tess of the Derby Villas, "we don't give two straws about coming through your bally gate. What we want is information."

Ethelred raised an eyebrow at her and asked, "Information?"

"Quite so," she said, "solid, reliable intelligence on the ground, unknown unknowns and all the rest. What we would like to know is, have you ever seen a palace about the place, and if you have, do please tell us where it is."

Hercules Potato added quickly, "It is assuming, *mam'zelle* Tess, the princess, she did not exaggerate her status in any way."

Turning back to Ethelred, he said, "It may be she lived in nothing more than a large house, which you might not be able distinguish one from another. To be more precise, we search for the home where lived a magnificent but impossible Borzoi. Have you ever seen such a dog come by here before?"

Ethelred, however, did not mean to be so easily converted into a fountain of information. "It may be," he ventured, "I have seen such a dog before, and it may be I have not."

"Great grieffers," said in Tess of the Derby Villas, "don't go playing that game old boy. It's too tiresome for words. Why can't you just snap to with a handy yes or no?"

Hercules Potato again intervened. "I understand, *monsieur* Ethelred, you are the dog most conscientious, you do not give away reports of your neighbors willy-nilly. Yes, I understand, it is most admirable of you."

Ethelred nodded appreciatively. His pink and grey bunny ears flopped above the gravely important expression on his face.

Tess of the Derby Villas muttered under her breath, "It's the darndest thing I ever saw in my life—a stern Labrador. It beggars every belief."

"It is a matter of urgent importance," said the famed detective, as he began to deliberately butter-up his witness. "The information we seek, it is a matter of hero and dog no less. This is why we came to you. You are well-known as a dog who knows about things that go on in this so lovely village."

Tess of the Derby Villas shot him a look of incredulity, but Ethelred, approving the statement, said, "It is always a pleasure, I am sure, to meet with a dog of sense. I can quite see that is what you are. I am held in high regard here in Market Gleaming, and it is my duty to my heroes to see to it the territory behind this gate is properly respected."

Tess of the Derby Villas rolled her eyes and made ready to offer a few more opinions about his gate, but Hercules Potato held up a cautionary paw to her and continued his line of questioning. "How good of you to notice I am a dog of sense, and I assure you, I am the famed detective with sense. What can you tell us then, most worthy and most ready Ethelred, of a magnificent but impossible white Borzoi?"

Ethelred still hesitated to accept this invitation to take leave of his scruples. He said, "She is a figure of some importance in this neighborhood, and I do not care to be the dog who casually chats up strangers with her goings and comings."

"*Oui, oui,* I understand. I too know that the Borzoi, she is *importante*. At least, I know she says so about herself. What I need to know is where does she come from? Where is the home of her hero? Her hero, you understand, has lost her, and we know where she is. This is, I emphasize again, a matter of hero and dog."

At last, Ethelred was ready. He indicated with his muzzle a direction down the lane to the left as he said, "She hails from just down that way. If you keep fast to the lane, go neither left nor right, it will end. You will see before you an impressive iron gate. I have never gone through it myself because it simply isn't done. Very rude it is to cross through another dog's gate, but that is where you will find the Borzoi's hero, if you are determined to be rude."

"Ah, *monsieur* Ethelred the most ready, you are an invaluable witness. I thank you, as does *mam'zelle* Tess, I am sure."

She just managed to mumble, "Oh yes, thanks awfully."

"Mind you," said Ethelred, "don't go putting it about you got any information from me. I have a reputation to uphold, and it wouldn't do for certain of the cats round here to get it into their heads I've become an easy mark." A pink and grey bunny ear flopped down over one of his eyes.

"*Non, non,* of course not," said Hercules Potato. "We will speak to no one of this secret interview, and now we will go on our way. Our case is nearly solved, and we must make the haste to go to this iron gate of which you tell us."

Ethelred nodded importantly as the famed detective and his bright and sporty assistant went on their way.

"Dash it all," exclaimed Tess of the Derby Villas as they trotted off. "I always thought Labradors were friendly, delighted chappies who would lay down the red carpet for one and all and every burglar, but this Ethelred in Bunny Ears goes wholly against type. I wonder what got into him along the way."

"Ah, the personality of a dog," explained Hercules Potato. "It is susceptible, as are all personalities, to the beautiful and to the ugly things of life. Past experiences create mysteries in everyone. *Monsieur* Ethelred, he is the good dog to his heroes, but his is not the mystery we are hoping to solve today, *mam'zelle* Tess. We are near, very near. Let us not lose our focus on a dog who goes about the in the bunny ears. In any case, you can believe me, you would prefer to have a chat with *monsieur* Ethelred the Ready more than you would with the sheep I encountered this morning.

Adventure-worn as they were, their journey at this point provided a pleasant atmosphere. Their paws clicked down an easy pavement, lined the entire way down with slender trees, encircled by plantings of pansies. Birds chirped above them, and the sounds of petite heroes at play sounded in the distance. It was a civilised place of heroes and animal life, and even if it turned out not to contain an actual palace, it was a fit enough place for any dog to live in.

"It's no Dale-On-Tweedy-Down," said Tess of the Derby Villas, "but it's nice all the same."

They proceeded on until they reached an intersection. The lane belonging to their pavement ended at this new road. Across it, a high brick wall rose up in front of thickly gathered, tall trees. Precisely in the center, closed and no doubt locked, the iron gate foretold to them by Ethelred rose upwards. From where they stood, the two dogs could see a drive leading steeply up from the gate and going deep into the trees.

"I rather think it's the one we want," said Tess of the Derby Villas.

"*Oui, d'accord,*" answered Hercules Potato. "It corresponds to the description given us by both Ethelred and by the princess herself. The gate, I see it is closed today, *comme d'habitude.* Still, I ask, why was it open on the day the princess chased after the scent of the chocolates?"

"I suppose it's possible they were left open accidently."

"Ah *oui, c'est possible,* accidents, they are always possible, but it would be a careless hero who left those gates open with a Borzoi free to run though them."

The two dogs bid their time while several motorcars zoomed past them. Once the street lay empty, they darted over to the other side and began a cursory round of investigative sniffs.

"*Mam'zelle* Tess," exclaimed Hercules Potato, "I smell the scent of the Princess Anastazia quite clearly here. Despite the rain, it is in every blade of these tufts of grass which clump around this gate."

Tess of the Derby Villas lept into the air, barking out her joy, but Hercules Potato shook his head in disapproval. "If you please, *mam'zelle* Tess, we must to remain calm, we must to remain focused."

Observing again the iron bars, he said, "It will not be a problem to slip through these bars. They may be highly esteemed, but I am glad it is not Cassius and Epimone who are here on this case to assist me, *mam'zelle* Tess. They would not be small enough to pass between these bars after me."

"And I am glad Ethelred is not here with us. I am in no mood for a lecture on gate etiquette." Tess of the Derby Villas shook herself vigorously, and as she squeezed in between the bars, she said, "I am sure he would denounce us both as determined slinkers."

"*Monsieur* Ethelred, he is ideological about the gates. Even if a dog wishes to cross a gate not his own in order to help another dog, *monsieur* Ethelred, he makes no distinctions. Myself, I agree with him partly. It is generally rude to cross gates, but sometimes the facts of the case make it necessary for a polite dog to do so. *Monsieur* Ethelred, he holds if it is wrong to cross the gate of another dog generally, it must therefore be wrong to do it under any circumstance."

"He's off his onion," said Tess of the Derby Villas as they made their way up the drive."

Hercules Potato shook his head, "*Mais non, Monsieur* Ethelred, he is hardly the first to be an ideologue. There was once a philosopher hero, a *monsieur* Kant, who was ideological in a different way. He insisted it is always wrong to tell the lies; only the truth may be spoken. *Normalement*, we all agree. Lying, it is wrong. *Monsieur* Kant, however, he did not make the distinctions."

"Our Ethelred to a tee," said Tess of the Derby Villas, as they continued up the incline.

"He proposed a hypothetical to explain his philosophy. Suppose, he said, he saw a hero fleeing for his life because a murdering antihero was chasing him and wanted to kill him."

"It's a dramatic picture, to say the least."

"Quite so, *mam'zelle* Tess. Well, *monsieur* Kant, he insisted that if the murdering antihero knocked on his door and asked him in which direction the fleeing hero had gone, it would be wrong for *monsieur* Kant to lie about knowing where he went."

"Great Scott, even though telling the truth would mean the poor fleeing hero would most likely be murdered?"

"*Oui*, according to *monsieur* Kant, even if it meant someone being murdered, it would be wrong to lie and to say he did not know where the fleeing hero went because it is always wrong to tell a lie. Our duty, he said, it is always to tell the truth. However, his ideological insistence left him blind to an alternative answer to his hypothetical."

"What's that, Potato?"

"The courage."

"Where does courage come into it?"

"Like so, *mam'zelle* Tess. When the murdering antihero asked, 'where has the fleeing hero gone?" *monsieur* Kant, he could have said, "I am not going to tell you."

"The murdering antihero might not like that answer very much."

"*Non*, but it too is the truth. *Monsieur* Kant could have saved the fleeing hero by truthfully insisting, come what may, he will not give any answer, if it means that another hero could be killed. Maybe the murdering antihero kills him instead, or maybe not. *Peut-être*, such demonstration of courage, might it not shame the would-be-killer into giving up his wickedness? We cannot know, but we would know for certain that *monsieur* Kant spoke the right and truthful answer."

"You know, Potato, you can be a bit of an ideologue yourself."

"How so? Please to tell, *mam'zelle* Tess."

"It's those scents and logic you are forever insisting on. In every situation, you will not allow that anything else could do the job as well or better."

"Mm, perhaps you make the good point, *mam'zelle* Tess. It is true that the scents and the logic, they were in the dereliction of the duty when the ghost of Thane Mortimer came calling. As long as no one uses the word, 'Magic," I will allow that the hope and the things spiritual, they have shown themselves to be more helpful than I previously believed them capable. Nonetheless, for the greater part of our case, it is the scents and the logic that have brought us to look upon the palace that stands before us now."

The crest of the incline had flattened out, and the trees parted into a giant circle going round immense grounds. The drive they stood on stretched forward, curving past an ornately sculpted fountain, and passing in front of the scene's pinnacle glory—an enormous, white palace, glittering beneath droplets of the recently fallen rain, while the luster of fresh sunshine shone down from above the now cloudless blue sky.

CHAPTER IX

THE PRESENTATION OF THE ROYAL CHEW TOY

"I say, it's a pile, all right," gasped Tess of the Derby Villas, marvelling at the immaculate grounds and the tremendous palace of the true hero. "Our magnificent but impossible Borzoi really does live in a bally palace."

She sat down for a moment and began to mentally process the

whole affair from beginning to end. "Humph, back in time for dinner indeed."

"Eh, what was that you said, *mam'zelle Tess?*" asked Hercules Potato, as he too sat down for a rest.

"Only that I call it a bit thick of the Colonel to have been so certain we'd be back in Dale-on-Tweedy-Down in time for our dinner on the same day we started out. Here we are, three days later, after a gushing rain, and only just now finding the object of our quest. A simple, four point plan, my back paw it was."

"It is exactly why I never shared with the Colonel his conviction that all would be so simple."

Tess of the Derby Villas had by no means finished her assessment. "Tragedy and disaster chased us the whole way here. You would think an experienced veteran of the Dogs of Dawn might have known better than to be so ruddy optimistic. Old Pruie's existential influenza is starting to strike me as a good deal more in keeping with the scheme."

"*Mais non, mam'zelle* Tess, *moi,* I do not think it is quite so bad. Where the Colonel and your friend, the dejected Prufrock, are concerned, they both stayed at home did they not? All they could do was to imagine for us how we would experience our case. We, however, know what it is to be out here in the thick of it. We have been neither doomed to failure nor assured of our success. We have had to recover from the guarantees that let us down, and to make the most out of the opportunities unexpected. It is, I think, what the hero philosopher Socrates meant when he once said of life, you can listen to what someone else tells you about something, or, you can go out and experience what it truly is for yourself."

He stood back up and shook himself out all over, and made what attempt he could to smooth out his bedraggled beard and moustache. Then he said, "Now, *mam'zelle Tess,* the royal chew toy, it is ready for its presentation at the palace?"

His bright and sporty assistant rose to all fours and reached back her muzzle to sniff at it. "It's as ship shape and Bristol fashion as its ever going to be."

"*Bien*, we will proceed across this lawn most magnificent and find, I trust, the true hero of the lost Princess Anastazia, he is at home."

The two confident and lighthearted dogs trotted across the velvety soft, immaculate lawn. The fountain made pleasant gurgling sounds, and bees buzzed in and out of the flowers that bordered the grounds' flawless edges. Splendour shone about them from every direction, and despite the hardships of the past few days, they could not help but feel delighted to be in such a place on such an afternoon.

They reached an impressive cascade of marbled front steps, and mounting these, they stood before the ornately carved double doors guarding the entrance to the palace itself. At this point, Hercules Potato realised they were at something of an impasse. Nature's caprice did not allow a Belgian Griffon, who stood a mere 35 centimeters from the ground, to ring a doorbell situated one meter above his head. There was nothing for it except to start barking.

"Jappe, Jappe, Jappe," he called out. He scratched on the baseboard to emphasise the urgency of his visit, then he continued barking, "Jappe, Jappe, Jappe."

Tess of the Derby Villas joined in, "Grr-rah, grr-rah, grr-rah."

After a short interval, one of the doors opened. The two small dogs looked up at a grand hero, clad in an impeccable, dark suit and pristine white gloves. He, in turn, looked down upon two small, impressively filthy dogs. If this scene took him by surprise, he did not show it. He only said, "I see."

Tess of the Derby Villas wagged her tail as a show of her friendly purpose, and then she boldly stepped forward, dipped her neck solemnly, and presented the royal chew toy tied to her collar to his full view.

"I see," said the grand hero again. He stooped down to have a closer look. "Upon my word."

A second voice filtered out from inside, asking, "Who's there, Monday?"

The grand hero in the dark suit and shining shoes straightened up again and answered over his shoulder, "Two dogs, my lord."

The second voice repeated, "Two dogs?"

Hercules Potato and Tess of the Derby Villas then saw a second hero's head pop up over the shoulder of the hero in the dark suit and shining shoes. This new hero said, "Just as you say, Monday, two dogs. What can they want I wonder?"

Hercules Potato sensed things were proceeding in a desirable direction when the hero called Monday, having untied the royal chew toy and removed it from Tess of the Derby Villa's collar, turned and showed it to the other hero. "They brought this with them, my lord."

"Why," gasped the hero My Lord, "they have the chew toy of the Princess Anastazia. Wherever did you two get hold of this prize?" He lowered himself to one knee to better inspect his two remarkable visitors. "I suppose they must have found it on the grounds somewhere."

"Unlikely, my lord. I found it tied quite expertly around one of their collars, almost as though someone sent it with them as a message to you."

"A message? Then it must be a message about the princess." The hero My Lord scrutinised the visitors intently. "Whoever it was sent you here, and wherever it is you've come from, you both look like you've been through the wars. I say, Monday, there are two collar tags here."

Reaching one hand down to gently stroke Hercules Potato's head, he took the tag in his other hand. "Come here old boy. Let's have a look at your tag, what about a telephone number eh? 'Hercules Potato,'" he read aloud. Then, he turned to his other guest and, inspecting her tag, he read out, 'Tess of the Derby Villas.' Ha! Someone's read his Thomas Hardy, eh wot?"

Standing up again and brushing his hand together, he said, "You two make a fine pair. However did you manage to find this chew toy? Do you know where to find the dog that goes with it?"

Here, his voice went quite wobbly, and he wiped a tear from his eye. Gazing into the distance, he said, "She is missing from me most dreadfully, you know, most dreadfully."

Hercules Potato and Tess of the Derby Villas locked excited eyes together. By his tears and sorrow, the true hero of the lost Princess Anastazia had revealed himself.

There might be two heroes in this palace, thought Hercules Potato, but it is clear to which hero the duty of the princess belongs.

The hero Monday placed a hand on the true hero My Lord's shoulder and said, "Steady yourself, my lord, she may turn up yet."

The true hero My Lord said, "Quite right, Monday, now how about our bringing these two dogs inside, and we will see about getting someone on the telephone who can tell us about them."

"They are rather dirty dogs, my lord."

"It's perfectly all right, Monday. Poor little devils, they must have been out of doors for days and could do with a touch of civilisation. I don't expect they will bring off any major damage while we find out what's what and the scoop of the day."

"Very good, my lord," said the hero Monday, and turning back to the dogs, he said, "If you will both follow me."

As Tess of the Derby Villas would later tell her friend Prufrock, "After three perfectly horrific days and the four point plan in the most shocking shambles, we entered that glittering palace as though we were visiting royalty. Of course, it would have been much more enjoyable if I hadn't been quite so filthy, but it was an absolutely smashing place."

As they came through, their paws felt the lovely plush of a red carpet. This ended at the foot of the entryway stairs and gave way to a stretch of polished marble floor. Tess of the Derby Villas, unaccustomed to ice-like conditions inside of doors, skidded halfway into the middle of the enormous foyer. The hero Monday observed the streaks of dirt left in her wake but stoically said nothing about it.

"Easy there, old thing," laughed the true hero My Lord. "I can't go sending you off back home with a lot of broken bones, now can I?"

The hero Monday walked over to a small table under an out-of-the-way alcove. Both dogs saw what was there.

"It is the sign most promising, *mam'zelle* Tess," whispered Hercules Potato. "The Colonel, he made a correct guess that these heroes would have a bizarre contraption, *n'est-ce pas?*"

The hero Monday said in a low, placid voice, "Come, Hercules Potato."

Hercules Potato cautiously picked his way across the slick marble floor. The true hero My Lord read out the number on his tag to the hero Monday, who pressed his forefinger on certain of the various buttons featured on the bizarre contraption. This then was the moment for the possibility of communication to shine or to collapse into ruin, and the two dogs anxiously awaited the result of the performance.

They listened as the hero Monday said, "Good day, Madam. I am speaking to you from Gleaming Hall, Sweepsbury. I have the Earl of Moppes on this end, may I enquire whom it is I am speaking with… Very good, his lordship desires to speak to you on a matter concerning some two dogs… Indeed, Madam, you heard me correctly, two dogs. May I put his lordship on the line with you?… Very good, Madam, thank you."

The hero Monday handed the bizarre contraption over to the true hero My Lord, who the two dogs now correctly intuited should more accurately be called the true hero Lord Moppes. The hero Monday said, "Mrs. Thistlewait is quite pleased to speak with you, my lord."

"Thank you, Monday," said the true hero Lord Moppes, as he took over the command of the bizarre contraption. Hercules Potato and Tess of the Derby Villas took a few anxious patters forwards. The Colonel's four-point plan, however badly it had worked out in practice, depended on this moment for its ultimate success.

Tess of the Derby Villas whispered, "Now is the time for the ole biz-con to work its magic."

Hercules Potato winced, but he kept his focus.

"Hullo, hullo, hullo, Lord Moppes here, I say though, just call me Jules. Jules Gules, viscount Nettoyer, that's what they used to call me at school you know... You did know? I was at school with your cousin? What a quiz... Yes, I remember old Squeaker, that's what we called him, took forever for his voice to change, course he ended up singing baritone, but the name had stuck by then so... Splendid. Right then, Mrs. Thistlewait, I will come straight to the point. I have two dogs here. They appeared quite out of the blue on my doorstep, out of nowhere, I tell you. The one attached to your number seems to be called Hercules Potato. Ring any bells?... You don't say?... Splendid, and the other one? The one called Tess of the Derby Villas?... How extraordinary."

Here, he cupped one hand over the lower end of the bizarre contraption and said to the hero Monday, "She doesn't know about the Derby Villa dog. It's not her's."

He returned to the line, and said, "Mrs. Thistlewait, I suppose I'd better get on to the other owner... Oh, you know them, do you?... I say, that's jolly good of you. I'm just going to bundle them into the motorcar with my man Monday here... That's right, the one you just spoke with, and he will bring them both round to you straightaway... Splendid."

Again he broke off from the conversation to say, "That's all right with you isn't Monday? You can handle taking two dogs on a drive to Dale-on-Tweedy-Down can't you?"

"Certainly, my lord."

"Dale-on-Tweedy-Down, Little Marchmain, it is, Mrs. Thistle-wait... I do know it, yes. I have a dear aunt who lives right there, Aunt Blevins, sweetest dear in the world... Oh you know her too?... She just popped off for several months holiday on a cruise round that world... Are you indeed? I say that is a first rate thing for you to do."

He broke off to say, "Monday, this Mrs. Thistlewait knows my Aunt Blevins."

Going back to the line, the true hero Lord Moppes said, "Well, you see, Mrs. Thistlewait, my old aunt died recently, Aunt Blevins' sister as it happens. I had to perform an errand that took me over to Dale-on-Tweedy-Down to see her... Yes, the living one, Aunt Blevins. As I said, I went to visit her quite recently, took a present over to her, but, of course, you know all about that don't you..."

Here he paused again and said, "You remember the way, don't you, Monday?"

"Yes, my lord."

Returning to the line, the hero My Lord said, "As I was saying, Mrs. Thistlewait, after my old aunt went off to join the great majority... Thank you, very kind of you to say, but she lived a full and long life. She always told me, 'Jules, my boy, when it comes time for me to hand in my portfolio, I'm going to leave it all to you,' and do you know, the good old egg was as true as her word. She left me the entire packet, right down to her blasted cat...Yes, well, I know some people are fond of them, but I am allergic. I have, or rather I am supposed to have a dog..."

Ears on the prick, Hercules Potato and Tess of the Derby Villas scooted in closer.

"Yes, I did say 'supposed to have.' It is all so impossibly sad you see. I lost my dog not four days ago... Yes, thank you for your condolences. I am smashed to bits over it, Mrs. Thistlewait, completely shattered... You are kind indeed to say so. She is the dearest thing to me in the entire world. I am a hopeless mess without the princess, but here's the most peculiar thing about this strange kettle of fish, or should I say strange kettle of dogs? No, something sounds off there, better go with the fish, but getting back to business, these two dogs here showed up on my doorstep with the princess' favorite chew toy tied around one of their collars... Absolutely they did..."

Here he shifted from the line again to say, "That's what you said, wasn't it Monday, the chew toy was tied about the collar?"

"Indeed, my lord."

"Mm, Mrs. Thistlewait says she doesn't know a thing about that."

He went back to the line. "What's that, Mrs. Thistlewait?... She is a magnificent, a most magnificent Borzoi, a giant white creature, absolutely magnificent, of course she can be quite impossible too, but I'd give anything... Say what?... You don't say?... Four days ago was it?... No collar?... That would be right, yes, I have the princess's collar here still... She had a chew toy with her when your neighbor found her? Hullo."

Here, the true hero Lord Moppes again covered part of the bizarre contraption with his hand and shouted, "Monday, you are never going to believe it, this Mrs. Thistlewait says her neighbor has the Princess Anastazia. I never would have thought she could have gotten away so far as that."

"Are they sure it is her, my lord?" asked the hero Monday, matter-of-factly indifferent to this world restoring revelation.

"Well no, but look here, it must be her. Dash it, if Aunt Blevins hadn't gone away when she did, she would have recognised the princess and had her back here the day she went missing."

He went back to the line. "Hello there, Mrs. Thistlewait? Yes, we're coming straightaway. Is your neighbor at home do you think?... Oh, would you? You are an absolute saint. Refresh my memory?... Capital, capital... The second lane off of the High Street... The fifth house on the left... tree swing in the front garden... Yes, Little Marchmain, beautiful front garden as I recall, by the way, splendid literary homage. We will be there within the hour... No, no, thank you, Mrs. Thistlewait. Cheerio, and see you in a jiffy's jiffy."

~

As the grand hero Gwendolyn replaced the bizarre contraption back onto its hook in the kitchen of Little Marchmain, Pookie Shams stood witness with the rest of the family to hear her miraculous words, "Hercules Potato is coming home."

Everyone had been gathered round her waiting with bated breath as they heard her side of the conversation unfold, and now the kitchen was filled with celebratory clamour.

"Brilliant," shouted the grand hero Gavin, "who found him?"

But his wife's answer disappeared into the noise of the two petite heroes each shouting in unison, Hooray! Hooray!" They jumped up and down, and every one hugged each other, followed by further whoops of "Hooray! Hooray!" Pookie Shams bounded up chairs and down chairs, and spun round multiple times in between, barking "Yip, yip, yippee." His tongue panted; his tail wagged, and his little shape shook end to end with happiness.

The petite hero Montcy, pausing from her jubilation to catch a few breaths, said, "Pookie Shams is excited too. He knows Hercules Potato is coming home."

The grand hero Gwendolyn bent down to stroke the panting, quivering little dog and said, "I think he is probably just excited because he sees all of us excited, but it is a happy day for everyone. Isn't it Pookie Shams? Hercules Potato is coming home. What a happy, happy day."

Pookie Shams, amidst the throes of joy, registered his singular accord with her statement by licking her face and panting still more.

AFTER RINGING off on his end, the hero Lord Moppes turned back to the hero Monday and said, "We'll leave just as soon as we've given these dogs some refreshment, Monday. Why, they must not have had any food for days. Take them into the kitchen and give them some water and see if you can't find them a few biscuits or something, eh wot?"

"Certainly, my lord, and shall I prepare the motorcar for departure as well?"

"Yes, Monday, quite right, get the motorcar out of the garage. We're going to bring the Princess Anastazia home again."

"*Tout finit bien, mam'zelle* Tess," whispered a self-satisfied Hercules Potato as they trotted off behind the hero Monday.

She whispered back, "It is an indisputable triumph of communication. Old Pruie will burst her modernist gasket when she hears about it."

"*Oui,* the case of the lost princess, it concludes most successfully," he said, and the two dogs clapped the tips of their tails together in celebratory cheer as they clicked over the marble floor at the heels of the hero Monday.

Later, Tess of the Derby Villas would say to Hercules Potato, "The true hero Lord Moppes is a kind enough chappie, but he comes off as rather a daft sort. I had a pickle of a time picturing the kind of hero who could attach himself to a dog as swollen-headed as her high-and-royal-mighty-ness the Princess Anastazia. Now I've met him, though, I suppose I can rather see them as happily matched."

Hercules Potato would answer her, "It is true what you say, *mam'zelle* Tess, and once they are reunited, may no ill chosen walk to investigate the scent of the chocolate ever again put true hero and true dog asunder."

∾

CHAPTER X

O HAPPY DAY! O HAPPY, HAPPY, HAPPY DAY

*T*he famed detective and his bright and sporty assistant made quick work of the water and biscuits the hero Monday placed before them. "A kind gesture, I'm sure," muttered Tess of the Derby Villas, "but if he truly wanted to air his gratitude, he might have tossed in some bacon."

However, a stomach filled with biscuits is to be preferred over a stomach filled with nothing at all, and the dogs happily took to the hero Monday's heels when he indicated a move out of doors was now expected of them.

Going out into the rear of the palace grounds, they made their way over a gravel drive leading towards the wood. Hercules Potato's nose jumped to alert. He whispered urgently, "*Mam'zelle* Tess, it is once again the scent at first so mysterious to me."

"I don't smell it," she whispered back.

"It is weak, but it is here all the same, and it is becoming stronger through these heavy trees. The rain, it could not wash everything away back here. *Non, non*, not everything." He sniffed intensely as another familiar scent mixed in with the one that interested him so. When they presently arrived at a garage beneath the shade of the trees, Hercules Potato whispered, "*Mam'zelle* Tess, do you smell nothing here that surprises you?"

"Well, no. I can't say as I do," she said, "but it's all jolly pleasant."

"We must just pass through here," said the hero Monday as he opened a door at the side of the garage. The two dogs followed after him, Hercules Potato sniffing meditatively as he went. They entered a small room where there was another door. Tess of the Derby Villas sneezed. The hero Monday said, "Bless you. I must apologise for the dust. This is something of a security station, but it is not often used. I am afraid I often neglect to send anyone in here to dust. If both of you will kindly remain here a moment, I will just warm up the engine of the motorcar."

He disappeared into the second door, and Hercules Potato said, "In this security station, *mam'zelle* Tess, do you not smell it? A smell we know well, it is here, and also the smell that has troubled me this whole case, it is here too."

"Well, I smell *la* Princess well enough, but I can't say I smell anything else worth mentioning." She jumped up on a nearby chair and then sprang onto a small counter. Three B.W.S.s were there. "Look at these, Potato."

"*Oui*, I too see. The boxes-without-smells, they show the palace and its grounds and the iron gate. It is most interesting. Tell to me, *mam'zelle* Tess, are there any buttons or knobs up there?"

"There is a large red button."

She was just lifting up a paw to press it when the hero Monday breezed back in and scooped her up. "We don't need to press that button just yet. There is a remote control in the motorcar which will allow us to open the front gate when we come to it." He placed Tess of the Derby Villas back on the floor. "This way now please."

As the two dogs followed the hero Monday into the garage, the famed detective whispered to his bright and sporty assistant, "Hercules Potato, he knows."

"Knows what?"

"He knows all."

"Bully for you, but do have a shufty at the motorcar."

A gleaming black motorcar stood idling in front of the open garage door. Observing the dogs' interested expressions, the hero Monday said, "I quite agree with you. It is a beautiful motorcar, the best I have ever had the privilege to captain."

He opened one of the rear doors as he said, "It is, as you might well recognise, a 1949 Cadillac Sedan. His lordship's aunt had it brought over here many years ago." He went over to a nearby cabinet, and opening it, he took from it a bath towel. This he crisply shook open with a flick of the wrist and laid it out across the rear seat. He turned to the dogs and said, "If you would now please mount."

Tess of the Derby Villas hurried forward and leapt into the rear seat, but Hercules Potato waited with dignified calm to be lifted in by the hero Monday. Having seen the two dogs comfortably settled, the hero Monday shut the door and rounded to the front of the motorcar to take up his position at the steering wheel. Tess of the Derby Villas had a difficult time containing her excitement.

"It's jolly nice," she whispered, as she darted back and forth smelling the old leather and examining the floorboard. "There is a lot of history here, so many smells telling old, old stories."

"*Oui, d'accord*, there are the scents many and interesting here, *mam'zelle* Tess, but do you recognise any of them?"

"Well, her royal impossibleness has been in here for certain."

"*Oui, c'est vrai*, and anything else?"

The hero Monday had by now guided the motorcar out of the garage, and it soon pulled up to the front doors of the palace. He descended the motorcar and once again opened its rear door. The true hero Lord Moppes skipped light heartedly down the marble steps, his fingers snapping in rapid rhythm and his face bearing a radiant expression.

He said, "Thank you, Monday," and slid enthusiastically into the rear seat to join the two dogs.

"You are most welcome, my lord," said the hero Monday, and then he closed the door and returned to the steering wheel. As he started the motorcar down the steep drive, he suggested, "Perhaps, my lord, the two animals would enjoy having a window rolled down?"

"That is a topping idea, Monday," said the true hero Lord Moppes.

He reached across to the window opposite him and put his hand on a gleaming chrome handle. As he rolled the window down, Hercules Potato and Tess of the Derby Villas, approved his plan and politely sniffed his arm. He brought the window just proud of the bottom, where it safely accommodated two dogs to let their ears blow about in the breeze.

"Right then, Monday," proclaimed the true hero Lord Moppes, "off we go. We have a princess to bring home."

The hero Monday reached up to the sunshade and flipped it

down, revealing a remote control. It was not a moment lost on Hercules Potato, Belgian Griffon and famed detective. He watched closely as the hero Monday pressed a button on it, and said with perfect confidence, "Open Sesame."

The iron gate at the base of the long, steep drive opened and permitted the dazzling black motorcar and its merry occupants to pass through into the lane. When the car was through the gate, the hero Monday pressed the button again, said, "Close Sesame," and the iron gates closed behind them. The famed detective thought to himself as they proceeded through the village at a low speed, *donc*, it is the moment decisive. My theory, it is proved correct.

Out of the window, the two dogs saw the familiar picket fence where Ethelred the Ready still stood to attention at his gate. His pink and grey bunny ears were no more. In the intervening time since they last saw him, one of his heroes had suited him up as a bumblebee.

"I never saw the like," muttered Tess of the Derby Villas.

Ethelred the Ready saw them and barked sharply, as was his wont, but even he could see clearly enough they meant to make no trouble about going through his gate. The two dogs in the motorcar barked back politely as they swept past him. Soon, they were headed along the open road at an exhilarating clip.

Hercules Potato and Tess of the Derby Villas thrust their small heads entirely out of the window and enjoyed the rewards of having done their faithful duty to dog and hero. Their ears flapping, their tongues streaming, they flew forward with the wind towards Dale-on-Tweedy-Down. Oh happy day was this, oh happy, happy, happy day.

"Hey, Mum," shouted the petite hero Lewis from the dining room, where he and Pookie Shams were keeping a lookout for the arrival of Hercules Potato. "Hey Mum," he shouted again.

The grand hero Gwendolyn calmly entered the room, and said, "What is it, dear? You know it's not polite to shout in the house. Come and find me if you need something."

"Oh right, sorry, but look here, out the window, the Airedale from across the street is in our front garden again. Do you think he knows anything about why Hercules Potato went missing, or that he is coming home?"

The grand hero Gwendolyn followed his gaze and saw the familiar dog sniffing around the lavender and the Portuguese laurel. "No, of course not, darling. He's just out wandering about. It's what dogs do. Now, do please go upstairs and brush your hair. I won't have you looking like a mangy dog yourself when Lord Moppes arrives."

"I thought he told you to call him Jules?"

"That's as may be, but as for you and Montcy, you are both to address him as Lord Moppes. Am I quite clear?"

"Okay, mum, but are you sure you got it right? Is it actually Lord Moppes?" In a singsong voice he rhymed, "Not a Lord Brooms, or Lord Dusters or whom? Sir Sweeps-A-Lot? He takes tea a lot, but not since he lost his mop to Sir Plumms-A-Rot."

"You are not one to miss the boat, are you, darling," said the grand hero Gwendolyn, stifling a smile as she shooed him out of the dining room. "No more being cheeky, and you go and brush your hair, just as I told you. See if you can't get that cowlick to stand down."

The petite hero Lewis bounded towards the staircase, but as he reached it, he turned around and said, "Hey Mum?"

"Yes, darling" she answered as she bent down to scoop Pookie Shams into her arms.

"It's such a happy day. I wish we had a present or something to give Hercules Potato when he gets here. Something just to show him how much we missed him."

"I think seeing you and Montcy will be the only present he will want, my darling," she said, leaning down and placing Pookie Shams in the hall passage.

The petite hero Lewis smiled and shouted, "Oh happy day," as he charged up the staircase making an almighty clattering.

The grand hero Gwendolyn stroked Pookie Shams' head and said, "A parade of elephants, executing 32 changements in a ballet class, would make less noise than our Lewis on a staircase."

The grand hero Gavin popped his head into the hall passage from the kitchen door and said, "Gwenda, love, the front garden is still soaked from all the rain we had earlier. Do let's try to keep everyone off of it, if we can."

"Naturally, dearest. I plan to receive Lord Moppes in the White Room, but I expect the dogs will be filthy. I simply don't want them coming into the house at all until they have had a bath. We can put them in the back garden with the children, don't you think?"

"Oh well, yes, as long as it's the back garden, that's the ticket," he agreed.

"It is a pity that it rained, Gavin dear. You didn't get to try out your sprinkler system."

"Oh well that is all right. The main thing is, it is set and fully operational. It will get its use, just you see."

Pookie Shams went to lie down on Hercules Potato's kitchen cushion to mull over a few things. The famed detective might insist that here reposed a puddled thinker, but just then, Pookie Shams was, in fact, deep in thought. Then, all of a sudden, he scampered up and made a mad dash for the dog's door. He had been struck with an inspired idea, and he made haste to realise it.

THE HAPPY TROUPE of heroes and dogs in the 1949 Cadillac Sedan, reached the valley where begins Dale-on-Tweedy-Down in due course. They cruised along until turning on the second lane off of the High Street. Then they passed gracefully beneath the elms and the oaks and the maples, arriving at wonderful last to the fifth house on the left, the one with the tree swing in the front garden.

The hero Monday turned off the motorcar's engine and said, "Little Marchmain, my lord."

From the window, the two dogs saw the Colonel, the celebrated leader of the Dogs of Dawn, pacing nervously back and forth in his front garden. Later, Tess of the Derby Villas would tell her friend Prufrock, "He looked just like that general the hero writer Mr. P.G. Wodehouse loved to mention. The one whose regiment charged the wrong hill, at the wrong time, on the wrong day of the wrong year, and well he might have done. The Colonel's plan was a mare's nest, even if it did work a treat in the end."

The hero Monday opened the rear door, and the two dogs tumbled out, followed by the true hero Lord Moppes. They all went happily through the front gate and up the reclaimed stone pathway. Hercules Potato felt certain the Hyacinths were glad to see him back, and even the weigela seemed unable feign disinterest.

The Colonel, of course, observed their every movement and lost no time in crossing the lane to follow them. He held back at the gate, only pressing it open with his nose enough to watch as the hero Monday rapped on the front door. He saw the grand heroes Gavin and Gwendolyn emerge and friendly greetings exchanged.

Next, the two petite heroes burst through the group and made an ecstatic show of welcoming back Hercules Potato. The grand hero Gwendolyn knelt down to pet him, and to give a bit of attention to Tess of the Derby Villas. Standing back up, she made emphatic gestures with her hands, and the petite heroes disappeared with the dogs around the back of the house. Everyone else went through into the house.

While the Colonel considered what his next move should be,

he saw the hero Jefferies coming up the lane with the Princess Anastazia on a lead. "Hello, hello, if it's not the Colonel." To the magnificent but impossible Borzoi at his side, he said, "He's come to see you off, my fine lady. Princess Anastazia? That's what Mrs. Thistlewait said they call you, isn't it?"

The Princess Anastazia answered with a deep, heraldic, "Ulyu-lyulyu! Ulyulyu!"

It rang out through the second lane, all the way into the High Street and out across the village to hand that held the sprawling valley at the foot of the high hill.

The Colonel quietly said, "Your royal highness, it has been an honour to serve you."

The front door of Little Marchmain flew open, and the true hero Lord Moppes burst out upon its porch. He gazed full upon the dog whose well beloved voice had called him hither from where he sat in the White Room. Hercules Potato and Tess of the Derby Villas came running from the back garden, the petite heroes with them.

"Princess Anastazia," spoke the hero Lord Moppes worshipfully as he stepped down from the porch. The hero Monday and the grand heroes Gavin and Gwendolyn all crowded in at the front door. It was a moment that none who stood witness to would fail to remember with awe for as long as they lived—the sight of a magnificent but impossible Borzoi taking flight from a single leap and streaming through the air into the arms of her true hero.

"My glorious heart, Pruie," Tess of the Derby Villas would later say to her friend, "it was the kind of thing poets write songs about, songs we sing when all is lost and we want to remember what beauty is before we die. Of course, the second she made contact, the *pas de deux* collapsed into a heap atop the busy Lizzies."

"Steady on," said the grand hero Gavin through a grimace. "Mind the flowers if you can please." The two petite heroes ran over to help untangle the princess from her lead, now wrapped around the true hero Lord Moppes' legs, while the grand hero Gwendolyn stooped down to assist him back to standing. "Dear me, Lord Moppes, ah, Jules, you aren't injured I trust?"

"Bless me, no. I'm not injured, not in the slightest, terribly sorry about flattening your busy Lizzies though," he said as he held up a fistful of flattened, torn flowers. He stroked the princess' head. "My own dear dog. I feared to never see you again."

The Colonel saw his moment and pressing the gate open, he went forwards into the front garden. Hercules Potato and Tess of the Derby Villas came up to meet him as he lept over the weigela, taking a few Hyacinth petals with him. The grand hero Gavin did not see this travesty occur, as his back was turned while he ushered his guests to take up seats on the front porch.

The Princess Anastazia took her place at the top of the porch steps and observed the scene below as one who is from on high. The petite hero Montcy went to the tree swing, and the petite hero Lewis went over to pet the Colonel. The grand hero Gavin called out, "Mind the garden, children. Don't go playing too hard on it. The grass is still quite wet and delicate after the rain."

"Okay, Pop," called the petite hero Lewis over his shoulder, and Montcy called out from the swing, "Don't worry, Daddy. My feet don't touch anything when I am on the swing."

Hercules Potato and Tess of the Derby Villas stood by while the petite hero Lewis petted the Colonel, who received his attention with a gracious lick and a waging tail.

The petite hero Lewis turned to his dog and said, "It's beastly rotten that dogs can't talk. You must have had a corking adventure. Could probably each do with a biscuit, eh? I tell you what, you wait here while I go scare some up."

After he went off, Tess of the Derby Villas said, "The lad's heart is in the right place, bless him, but I've had just about all I can take of biscuits. What a dog wants at a time like this is bacon."

The Colonel said, "Enough about bacon, Derby Villa. I have been waiting days to hear a report from you two. I started to wonder if you had chucked the whole thing in and decided to take a holiday instead."

"That's a fine thing to say," said Tess of the Derby Villas. "You had a cozy time of it here, but it may interest you to know we were out there in the dashed absolute wild, executing what I can now tell you was nothing short of a four-point disaster."

Hercules Potato said, "*Oui, c'est vrai*, it was a case most arduous, Colonel."

"So I have been hearing," said the Colonel. "The very shady Tabby cat MissTree began putting it round just this afternoon that you were both a washout, but not knowing where she got her information from, I didn't put much stock in it. What's this about the plan going to sixes and sevens?"

Tess of the Derby Villas said, "It went higgledy-piggledy directly we shifted from this front garden."

The Colonel, incredulous, turned to Hercules Potato to hear further explanations.

"It is true what *mam'zelle* Tess tells to you, Colonel. It was a case most arduous and trying upon the nerves."

Hercules Potato had not yet been granted an audience with the Princess Anastazia. He saw her now, sitting regally on the front porch, her true hero at her side. Upon seeing him, the magnificent but impossible Borzoi, benevolently favoured the famed detective with a nod of her noble muzzle. He supposed she rarely ever bestowed such royal gesture upon rank and file canines. It must, he thought, be the aforementioned royal remembrance. *Donc*, it is just as useless as I thought it would be, but at least we enjoyed the so nice ride in the motorcar.

The celebrated leader of the Dogs of Dawn was just saying, "I was nearby, sniffing around the hero Jefferies' back garden, when I saw him on the screened-in porch, fumbling with his bizarre contraption. I came closer and listened. I heard him talking about the news that the true hero of the princess had been discovered, which is when I knew MissTree must have been getting up a misinformation campaign. Good. Potato and company, you've brought the whole thing off with tremendous success, just as I knew you would. Though, as I said, I had thought you would be a little more expeditious in wrapping the campaign up."

Hercules Potato said, "The four scents, they did not queue up neatly end to end, as I warned you they would not, Colonel, but we found a few helpful and not so helpful witnesses here and there along the way. There was even a ghost dog. I still cannot explain how he was possible. There was nothing about him the scents or the logic could explain to me, yet there he was, involving himself in our case. He spoke to us, and he gave to us much worthwhile information."

"It strikes me as being all to the good, Potato," said the Colonel. "It's about time you learned there are more things in heaven and on the earth than are dreamt of by your scents and logic. As I am sure you know, every plan of attack is bound to have a hiccup or two. You know the old military maxim, 'order, counter-order, disorder.'"

Hercules Potato growled slightly as he said, "*Non*, Colonel. We were not knowing of this maxim, as you say. If you please, the next time you desire to plunge us into a goat song, you might consider apprising us of any more worthy expressions such as you may know before the tragedies hidden in your plan get going."

The celebrated leader of the Dogs of Dawn retorted, "When a plan of attack produces a rousing success without a single causality, it is the usual thing for the troops to sing and salute the dog who thought it up. They do not typically pepper him ungratefully with some of the more trifling incidents of the skirmish. I say, where is the sack I sent you off with, Derby Villa? The one you kept the royal chew toy in?"

"Oh, that," she answered with an unconcerned shrug, "we lost it ages ago. As it was, we did a marvellous job not losing the royal chew toy."

"Now that is badly done," exclaimed the Colonel. "My hero made that sack with her own two hands, and she'll miss it to be sure. What then? Really, I do wish you hadn't been so impossibly careless."

Tess of the Derby Villas would later say her friend Prufrock, "There are certain times in one's life, Pruie, when indignation touches one's soul so profoundly it renders all previously invented words largely useless for the purpose of expression. All a dog has left to her in such a moment is to express her uncowed spirit with a round of righteous barking."

Tess of the Derby Villas let go on the Colonel with her most vehement "Grr-rah! grr-rah! grr-rah," and Hercules Potato joined her with a resolute, "Jappe, jappe, jappe." Causing the Colonel to take a few bewildered steps backwards, and the weigela lost a few blooms as his backside collided with it.

Meanwhile, the Lady Stella, who had wandered out for a late day stroll, was just passing by the fifth house on the left, the one with the tree swing in the front garden. Smelling the telltale scents of a notable gathering of heroes and dogs, the much admired beauty tested her muzzle on the front gate and, finding it unlocked, pushed it opened a crack to see what glad scene was then unfolding behind it.

Pookie Shams too returned from his errand just at this moment. He charged through the Portuguese laurel with a giant rat crammed between his jaws. Running up to Hercules Potato, who was still engaged with Tess of the Derby Villas in a volley of outraged barks against the Colonel, he presented his gift to his friend as a welcome home present. He wagged his tail and dropped the freshly killed rodent at the famed detective's front paws. He licked his friend's face then added his own, "Yip, yip, yippie."

Hercules Potato stopped barking and observed the rat. Pookie Shams waited expectantly for a show of approval. The famed detective's ego had taken so many blows over the last few days, that Pookie Sham's proud display of ratting talent was not the soul shattering event that he had always before felt it to be. Hercules Potato said, "*Merci*, Pookie Shams," and Pookie Shams licked him again.

The Colonel leaned in to inspect the rat, but Hercules Potato began barking at him again, until he noticed a moment later the Lady Stella's presence on the reclaimed stone pathway. He went several shades paler beneath his beard and moustache. He presented, he knew, a disgracefully disheveled figure. He sank down mortified and wondered if there was possibly a way for him to hide underneath the dead rat.

The petite hero Lewis was just coming across the grass with a bag full of biscuits when the petite hero Montcy saw the dead rat. "Rozie," she screamed as she jumped down from the tree swing, accidentally crushing a hosta growing near the tree's trunk.

The petite hero Lewis saw the rat next and exclaimed, "Coo." Then again, "Coo."

The grand hero Gwendolyn, noticing a commotion, came down from the porch. She too saw the rat, and she too fell to screaming, "Rat, it's a rat, Gavin. It's a dead rat."

The cry of the word "rat," secret code word that it was, sent out the command the fully operational sprinkler system had been eagerly waiting to hear all day. At their appointed intervals, four sprinkler heads shot up from the ground, rotated twice, then began to shower the already sodden grass and plants with a surplus dousing.

As the mud began to slicken, the petite hero Lewis, still moving towards the dead rat, lost his footing on the turf beneath him. He slid across the grass, his heels ploughing into it a long, thick gash. In trying to regain his footing, he fell again, and this time his topple crushed a swath of lavender growing along one side of the Portuguese laurel. The biscuits in the bag he had been carrying flew out everywhere.

The Lady Stella, not minding about the front garden having transformed itself into a dancing fountain, trampled several Hyacinths in her endeavour to leap over the weigela in order to sample the snacks. Several chrysanthemum buds also fell casualty to her pursuit of this object.

Tess of the Derby Villas had lept to the other side of the reclaimed stone pathway to avoid a sprinkler, but she landed on the loose stone the grand hero Gavin had not gotten round to tending to yet. It flew up backwards, hitting the grand hero Gavin full in the face as he rushed down from the front porch. The other dogs were alternately dodging a sprinkler, or diving for a biscuit, their paws ripping out tufts of grass and their tails knocking out any flower petal within striking distance.

Hercules Potato, hoping to save the last scrap of his dignity, attempted to avail himself of the miracle bath spurting up from the earth. However, with all of the mud slinging about, it did not, in the end, do him much good.

The grand hero Gavin, still smarting from the blow of the

flying piece of reclaimed stone, and with one hand held to his face, attempted to make a move towards turning off the sprinkler system. As he passed by the grand hero Gwendolyn, however, she snatched at his elbow and gasped, "The rat, dead rat. Get it out of here."

This threw him off balance completely and as he fought to regain his footing, his feet tore sizable chunks out of the grass. Then, he over balanced and pitched headlong into the weigela. His wife would have tried to help him back up to his feet, but just then, she saw the petite hero Lewis reaching down for the dead rat.

She screamed, "No, Lewis, don't touch it."

As she trampled over more Hyacinths to stop him picking up the dead rat, she tripped over Hercules Potato, who had been washing out his beard and moustache and did not see her coming. She stumbled and grabbed the petite hero Lewis for support, but they both went down together, sliding once more through the grass and contributing to it a twin gash to match the one Lewis had already donated to it. To add insult to injury, they made a crash landing into what remained of the lavender.

The petite hero Montcy sat sobbing under a spray of water because the petite hero Lewis, thwarted from touching the dead rat, began leaping and splashing about in the mud and muck chanting, "Rozzy Rat has spied her last, gone an died as bad outcast, Rozzy Rat has spied her last—"

The true hero Lord Moppes stood on the porch with the Princess Anastazia, gaping at the spectacle of ungainly motion, spurting water, and flying flower petals. Meanwhile, the hero Monday slipped quietly away to see what he could do about at least shutting off the water works performance.

Just as the front garden of Little Marchmain made its final plunge into a raving spectacle of tumult and chaos, the hero Sir Wordsworth Plumm happened along the pavement with the highly esteemed Vizslas, Cassius and Epimone, by his side.

"My hat, what a picnic," he observed as they walked by. As they passed on from the scene of active devastation, he said to his dogs, "These goings on at Little Marchmain fix things rather neatly for the Plummley Hall garden. We will be quite without competition for the Best & Beautiful. No doubt but it's a sad day for poor Thistlewait. Still, I cannot help but rejoice in our good fortune. Oh happy day indeed, for our own fair garden."

CHAPTER XI

HERCULES POTATO CLOSES HIS CASE

*I*n the latter calm of the post-dystopian scene in the front garden at Little Marchmain, the grand hero Gavin took the devastation of his beloved front garden with astonishing equanimity. His first concern had been to stop the petite hero Montcy sobbing herself silly over the dead rat, and to get her and her brother into dry clothes.

This, however, could not be managed until the petite hero Lewis had been made to assure his sister how impossible it was for the dead rat to have actually been her revered Rozzy Ratzo. He was made to further assure her the odds were even against its being any relation at all to the spy who does everything for Queen and country.

"After all, how could it be her?" said the grand hero Gavin. "Old Rozzy spends all of her time spying on the continent. It's most unlikely she would ever find any space for a visit to our quiet village."

Once she was dry and put into clean clothes, the petite hero Montcy readily accepted this version of the facts, and as they shepherded several dripping wet dogs into the back garden to dry out, she said, "Daddy, your beautiful garden is ruined. Are you dreadfully upset?"

"Thank you, my Montcy, your sympathy touches my heart, but there is always autumn, you know. I won't be able to make it into anything worth seeing until at least that long. I am afraid it rather leaves the way clear for Sir Wordsworth Plumm to run away with first prize at the Best & Beautiful."

"It isn't fair. He wins it every year."

"Oh, let him enjoy it. Come Michaelmas, we are going to be back up to snuff and taking first prize in the Autumn Foliage Fete. We'll give them as robust a show of crimson and gold as they never before saw, and we'll make old Sir Plummy think about chucking in gardening for some relaxed, indoor kind of hobby."

"I can help you," offered the petite hero.

"I say, my Montcy, that is just the bit I want most."

The heroes from the palace had taken their leave. After the hero Monday deftly turned the sprinklers off, he quietly took the Princess Anastazia by her lead and settled her in the motorcar.

The hero Jeffries shook hands with the true hero Lord Moppes, and the 1949 Cadillac Sedan returned to Gleaming Hall.

Though the heroes of Little Marchmain stoically accepted the fate of their front garden, other repercussions from the unfolding of events could not be taken so casually.

"Not in any home where I live," were the precise words of the grand hero Gwendolyn when she declared her refusal to take dead rats in her front garden lying down. After issuing orders for the dogs to be quarantined outside until they could be properly bathed and dried, she made Pookie Shams sit on the front porch while she scoured his teeth with an old toothbrush. The grand hero Gavin was tasked with removing the dead rodent via a shovel to parts unknown.

Following these proofs of her determination, she announced they were carting Pookie Shams off to the veterinarian post-haste. "We must insist he gets tested for rodent born diseases. I'll not risk the whole village demanding I keep my children home from school because one of our dogs brought home bubonic plague."

Hercules Potato shuddered at the thought, but the petite hero Lewis began to dance around the devastated front garden as he sang, "Ring a-round-the-rosies, pocket full of posies, ashes, ashes we all fall dead."

Pookie Shams joined right in with him. Yipping happily, the dog registered no concern at the grim hypothesizing that saw him as patient zero in a medievalesque contagion. The grand hero Gavin returned and scooped Pookie Shams into his travel crate, and off they all went to see him submitted to a medical examination.

Meanwhile, a crowd of dogs filed into the back garden of Little Marchmain. Word of the closing of the case had gone round the village, and all of its dogs wanted to hear the story straight from the famed detective's mouth. The grand hero Gwendolyn had thoughtfully supplied the wet dogs with some old towels, and once Hercules Potato felt restored to some degree of comfort, he felt ready to meet their expectations of him.

To the gathered circle, he said, "*Attention*, we are not alone. For there is *mam'zelle* MissTree skulking about on the tree branch overhead. Come down *mam'zelle*, and we will tell to you also what we know."

An incensed meow, followed by the shaking and rustling of tree leaves, produced the impenitent cat into their midst.

"Why He-rrrr-cules Potato" purred MissTree striding forwards, "you are a muddy-meddled rascal. Not allowed indoo-rrrr-s, are you now?"

Hercules Potato said stiffly, "*Mam'zelle* MissTree, I have had the shower, and now I have but the wet fur, and it will soon dry. There is not the muddy meddle, as you say."

The Lady Stella said, "Several of us look less than our best after the lawn became the mud slide. I think, *bien sûr*, that *monsieur* Potato, he looks very well. One must consider he spent a long three days without the things basic that a dog should have."

Hercules Potato blushed beneath his damp beard and moustache, but he found sufficient voice to say, "The Lady Stella, I thank you."

MissTree scoffed under her breath and said, "I was there, and I witnessed you having a te-rrrr-ible time on your little adventu-rrrr-e, Potato. You were very untalented." Her tail glided insipiently back-and-forth as she fixed her eyes on the Colonel and said, "Even this dog here believes no truly gifted detective would have taken so long to solve a case so simple."

The Colonel blustered and coughed and said, "Now, now, I was just a bit hard on them for taking their time. In the end, they came through, and they did their duty just as I expected of them."

Tess of the Derby Villas said, "What you see before you, my fine fellow dogs, is a cat who is nothing better than an attempted murderess."

Several shocked gasps, a few "tut, tuts" and one "dear me," met this accusation of guilt, but MissTree said insouciantly, "All I did was th-rrrr-ow a disgusting chew toy into the rrrr-iver, didn't I now? You are the one who chose to go in afte-rrrr it."

Tess of the Derby Villas was ready to tear into the cat, but a restraining paw held her back. The highly esteemed Vizslas, Cassius and Epimone were at her side.

"My beautiful friend," spoke Epimone gently, "let not your temper strike out at this unfortunate cat."

"No indeed," affirmed her brother Cassius, "let her be, and let us hear the full story from our famed friend, Hercules Potato. Sir, our ears belong to you. Speak to us."

Hercules Potato nodded to him graciously, and began, "The case, it was this way. The Princess Anastazia, she tells to us her misfortune is simple. She tells to us it resulted from the scent of the chocolate. Ah, but to everyone here I say again, Hercules Potato, he knows. He knows it cannot be so simple as this, and the scents and the logic, they prove him correct. Now for the truth of what happened."

He settled down comfortably into the folds of his towel and continued, "When the Princess Anastazia became lost after following the scent of the chocolate, it was not the thing called an accident. It was, as they say, the thing done with the malice afore-thought."

"What's that Potato," said the Colonel starting up.

"Please Colonel, I will bring you there with out delay." Turning back to the cat, Hercules Potato said, "*Mam'zelle* MissTree, it was not so long ago you came to live here in Dale-on-Tweedy-Down with the curiosity Blevins, *n'est-ce pas*? Please to tell us, where did you reside before this event?"

The very shady tabby cat said, "You a-rrr-e the famed detec-tive, you tell me."

"*Bien sûr*, I did not think to wonder at the time, but the more this case progressed, the more I did wonder about it. The more I wondered about the information you, *mam'zelle* MissTree, gave to me."

"I, give you info-rrrr-mation, Potato? Su-rrrr-ely you jest. I gave you no such thing."

"Ah, but *mam'zelle*, MissTree, you did, without meaning too, of course. When I spoke to you while you sat up in the tree, you told to me you followed part way the journey of the princess into Dale-on-Tweedy-Down. You did not say you followed 'a lost dog,' *non*. You said you followed 'the princess,' but how did you know then of her calling herself a princess? The Colonel, he kept this information secret. Colonel, you will remember when I asked the Princess Anastazia if the cat next door had been by to bother her?"

"Yes, naturally I remember, and she said she had not seen a cat since she had arrived, and she insisted she never speaks to them on any account."

"*Oui*, that is also as I remember it. So, if you knew then, *mam'zelle* MissTree, she was called a princess, you knew by some other means than by talking to her after she arrived in the village, nor did you hear about her being called a princess from anyone here in the village."

MissTree sat down and began to preen about her neck with a paw, coolly saying, "So I happened upon a derisory term for her that just happens to be what the beastly thing calls herself. It proves nothing."

Hercules Potato continued, "Also, you said to me you saw her with the chew toy. This confirmed to me you were not lying when you said you followed her into Dale-on-Tweedy-Down. The scents too, they confirmed you did indeed follow her part of the way into the glen. Your scent, it disappeared before we reached the graveyard, where we found the scent of the dead roses. *Donc*, it seemed then what you said was true. Yes, it could well have been the case that you were merely lurking about in the thicket when you spotted and began to follow the Princess Anastazia. It may have been true, even though *mam'zelle* Tess, she rightly pointed out to me that you are one who prefers to tell the fibs."

"It's a known fact," said Tess of the Derby Villas. "She is a walking, talking load of old cobblers."

Hercules Potato said, "So it is, *mam'zelle* Tess, for I shall now show that it was a lie after all. When first we came to the graveyard, I thought to myself, we must pass on to the next scents. The scent of *mam'zelle* MissTree will no longer be around, so why think any more of her?"

"Why indeed?" asked the cat.

"Because I now know you followed the Princess Anastazia the whole way from the palace to Dale-on-Tweedy-Down," answered the famed detective. Here, he paused to let this stunning revelation have its proper effect on his hearers. Seeing so many pairs of wide-eyed dogs staring back at him in rapt attention pleased the famed detective to no small degree.

He resumed his summation. "When a new scent first emerged near the graveyard, going along in the trail of the scent of the princess, I puzzled over it. When I continued to find it mingling near the scent of the chickens, and later too at the scent of the fish, I did not discount its importance as a clue."

"*Monsieur* Potato," implored the Lady Stella, "what was this scent? You must no longer leave us in the suspense."

"*Bien sûr*, but first, let us go back to the beginning. What is known about the case when it begins? It is known it was the habitual practice of the heroes at the palace to keep the front gate closed. It is always closed, unless the motorcar approaches it. There is, I saw for myself, the thing called the remote control. It sends a signal from inside the motorcar, and with the words, 'Open Sesame,' the iron gates open. After the motorcar goes out of the gates, the remote control and the words 'Close Sesame,' shut the gates."

"A wondrous happening," said the highly esteemed Vizsla Epimone.

"Indeed, it sounds most magical, sister," said Cassius.

"*Non*" said Hercules Potato. "There was not the magic, please to understand. It is in fact very logical the way this system operates. As for the case, it struck me as most curious that the scent of the chocolate drifted into to the nose of the princess just at the precise time this gate was inexplicably open. Then, when I am at the palace, I hear the true hero Lord Moppes say into the bizarre contraption that his deceased aunt was a curiosity aunt."

He paused again to ensure everyone followed his narrative. "When she was alive, living in the palace, she kept with her there a cat. When she died, she left everything, including this cat to her nephew, the true hero Lord Moppes. Ah, but what did he say, *eh?* He says he not only knows where Dale-on-Tweedy-Down is, but he knows the very lane to go to. He says he went to this lane recently to perform an errand, to bring to his aunt, the curiosity Blevins, a present."

Tess of the Derby Villas said, "I recall him mentioning to the biz-con that his good egg aunt left him the lot, even down to her cat."

"*Oui*, just as *mam'zelle* Tess reports. This is an important clue. His aunt dies. She leaves him a cat, but he does not want it. He is allergic to cats and he has already the dog. There is no cat at the palace these days, but the scent of a cat is still there in a few places, including in the so nice motorcar. So, from all of these facts, the scents and the logic, they allow me to infer that the gift the true hero Lord Moppes brought to his curiosity Aunt Blevins, it was a cat."

Tess of the Derby Villas said, "Are you saying what I think you are saying, Potato?"

"*Oui, mam'zelle* Tess, the scent of this cat, it was not inside the palace, it has been cleaned too well and too often, but when we went with the hero Monday to the rear grounds of the palace, there it was I could smell it. You will remember I asked you, 'do you not smell a scent familiar to you?' Both in the garage and in the motorcar?"

"I did, but it was the scent of the princess."

"*Oui*, that is true. I too smelled her there, but my nose, it is the nose for smelling the scents, and I smelled another besides the one belonging to the princess. It was the scent of *mam'zelle* MissTree."

More gasps of shock emitted from the circle of dogs.

"The hero Monday, he shows to us the security station. It is still in operation, but it is not often used, it has the dust floating everywhere. As it is rarely cleaned, the scents stay longer there than they do in the palace itself. Before I see anything, I smell it. I smell the scent of MissTree the cat. It was not the smell of a passing visit, *non*. It was the smell of the cat ensconced. What is more, the scent of MissTree the cat went side by side with the other scent so puzzling, and it is then that Hercules Potato, he understands all."

"You do keep saying that, Potato," said MissTree, "but for a dog who knows eve-rrr-ything, you say a lot of nothing, don't you now?"

"You, *mam'zelle* MissTree, were the cat who lived with the curiosity aunt at the palace. While she lived, the palace was your home. When she died, perhaps you were sad or perhaps you were not. You are a cat, so who can say? One thing is certain: you considered the palace to belong to you. However, a new world order unfolded at the palace *n'est-ce pas?* The true hero Lord Moppes, he became the one to decide what will be the scheme of life there. He decides it will not be one with a cat in it."

"You and your ti-rrr-esome hero worship disgust me," said the very shady Tabby cat.

Hercules Potato paid her no mind. He said, "He and the hero Monday, they take you into the motorcar one last time, and they drive you, all those many months ago, into Dale-on-Tweedy-Down.

They take the second lane off of the High Street. The motorcar goes past the fifth house on the left, the one with the tree swing in the front garden and the home of Hercules Potato, famed detective. They come to a stop at the home of the curiosity Blevins, the other aunt, the living aunt of the true hero Lord Moppes. She is ready and willing to be kind to you, and the heroes leave you with her, thinking you to be amply and generously cared for—which you were and are."

"The Blevins creature cleared out, didn't she now?" said Miss-Tree. She licked her paw and added, "not so very ca-rrr-ing a thing to do, is it now?"

"The curiosity Blevins is a worthy personage, and it is not wrong for her to take a holiday," said Epimone.

Cassius added, "She has always done kindly by all and for all. Did she not make the proper arrangements for you in her absence?"

Hercules Potato said, "She did indeed, but to return to the case, life with the curiosity Blevins did not suit you, did it *mam'zelle* MissTree?

"Why should it," asked the cat, dispassionately.

"*Non*. You desire to be back at the palace, *n'est-ce pas*? You desire the palace should once again be the home of a cat, a cat who does not share it with a dog. *Donc*, on many days, you return there to wait and to watch. The moment, it must be perfect, and it might take time to come to you. You make certain, however, you do not wait and watch from where you will have no power. Whenever you are there, you seat yourself at the little used but still fully functioning security station. All views of the grounds are visible to you there on the three B.W.S. Also visible to you is the front gate."

"Too true," said Tess of the Derby Villas. "The B.W.S. showed the entire scene."

"For many months, when you were able to make your visit there, you could accomplish nothing," said Hercules Potato. "Always, you are forced to return to the curiosity Blevins. Still, you keep to your course. Then one day, luck arrived at just the moment you wished for it. From where you sat in the security station, you saw the Princess Anastasia alone, without her collar. You saw her begin to chase after something in the direction of the front gate. The moment you desired had arrived. You pressed the red button that opens the front gate from the security station, *et voila!* The princess, she went through it and was gone."

"Upon my word, it's worse than I ever imagined," said the Colonel.

"As I said, Colonel, it was the thing done with the malice aforethought, but I return to the explanation of other scent, the one I first smelled at the graveyard and that was a mystery to me. At the moment when the princess rushed out of the open gates, it was also the moment when the known scent of *mam'zelle* MissTree the cat changed into this mysterious unknown scent."

"You tell of a hoax only a fai-rrr-ytale could swallow," said MissTree, her demeanour continuing calm.

"*Mais non,* it is not the hoax, it is how the scent works upon a personality," said the famed detective. "I remember such a thing happening to one of my own heroes. The grand hero Gavin, he has his own particular happy scent, except when he is unhappy about something in his front garden. I remembered how he smelled when his weigela was drooping. The scent of his unhappiness so changed his smell, that I would not have known it was his scent if I had not been there to see him smell so myself."

"*Incroyable,*" said the Lady Stella. "*Monsieur* Potato, you have indeed the amazing mind."

The famed detective blushed again, and it was a struggle to retake his narrative. He mastered himself, however, and continued on. "We return now to you, *mam'zelle* MissTree. *Normalement,* yours is the scent of the cat who smells of the fuming malady, of the ill temper, and of the mendaciousness. We all know that this is your scent."

At this, all of the dogs nodded their heads in agreement.

Cassius affirmed, "It is well said," and Epimone finished, "and we stand in agreement with your observation, good Hercules Potato."

He continued. "As you watched the Princess Anastazia running out of the palace grounds, and you saw your long waited for plan was working to perfection, you became for the first time a gleeful cat. It made you so happy that it changed entirely how you smelled. In the security station, you left behind you the one scent of your malady and the other scent of your glee. It was this scent of your glee, of what you no doubt call the happiness, that you left in your trail all along the way as you followed after the princess to see where she would go."

"Amazing," broke in Tess of the Derby Villas. "When exactly did you work all this out, Potato?"

"I did not know of *mam'zelle* MissTree's connection with the palace until after we had been to it, but I first solved the problem of the mystery scent just after you were nearly drowned, *mam'zelle* Tess. When I spoke with *mam'zelle* MissTree at the rushing river, I recognised straight away that the mysterious scent that had puzzled me was emanating from her at that exact moment. You were happy then as well, were you not, *mam'zelle* MissTree? You believed without the royal chew toy, and without my bright and sporty assistant, I would not be able to solve my case, *n'est-ce pas?*"

"I confess I was elated and no mo-rrr-e. I had disposed of that ho-rrr-ific chew toy, and though I had not thought of getting rrr-id of your assistant, her deciding to throw herself away on a slobbery knot of vile rrr-ags was a nifty little bonus, wasn't it now?"

"You are a thoroughly fermented rotter," cried Tess of the Derby Villas jumping up from her seat on the grass, but Hercules Potato held up a front paw and said, "*S'il tu plait, mam'zelle* Tess, if I may finish with my summation of the case."

His assistant sat back down begrudgingly, as he said, "I knew from at least the bank of the river, that *mam'zelle* MissTree had followed the princess all the way to the graveyard. I also knew that while she followed her, she had been a happy cat. This proved she had indeed lied from the beginning. She had not begun to follow the princess from a thicket near the glen. She had followed her for much longer a time. Had it not been for the rain and the work of the moles, I would have been able to trace our way to the palace by following only the scent of the gleeful cat, *mam'zelle* MissTree."

"Potato, the depravity shocks me," said the Colonel, shaking his head in disbelief.

"*Oui*, Colonel, it is a sad story of the envy, *n'est-ce pas*? I asked myself why it was *mam'zelle* MissTree became so happy as the princess chased scent after scent? Why did it make her so happy to see our intention to restore the princess to her true hero so nearly ended at the river? I knew she said it made her happy to watch us chase our case unsuccessfully. Later, I learned from *mam'zelle* Tess that she had deliberately sabotaged the chew toy."

"She cannot deny it," affirmed Tess of the Derby Villas.

"It could not, I was convinced, be merely due to her selfish propensity to delight in the misfortunes of others. *Non*, she wanted the place of the princess in the palace for herself," said Hercules Potato. "It was when I heard the true hero Lord Moppes talking into the bizarre contraption, and when I smelled the scent of the happy *mam'zelle* MissTree in the security room, that I knew that she was responsible for all that happened."

"*Donc*, she was in the security room, and she opened the gate with the red button," said the Lady Stella. "Then she followed the princess all the way to Dale-on-Tweedy-Down?"

"I am he-rrr-e, aren't I now?" said MissTree, standing up on all fours, her tail gliding back and forth, not the least bit agitated. "I am he-rrr-e, but I do not admit I was ever the-rrr-e. I am not in the habit of being made to break down and confess by a dog who cannot even catch so much as a rrr-at."

Hercules Potato held his head high and finished his summation, "*Mam'zelle* MissTree, you left the security station and raced to follow where the Princess Anastazia would go. Along all of the paths she took chasing the scent of the chocolate, the scent of the fish, the scent of the chickens, and the scent of the dead roses in the graveyard, you followed her and you left your happy scent behind you. You were still happy as you watched the Princess Anastazia wander about in the graveyard, but after she left it, and as she began to approach the thicket, the scents indicate that your mood darkened again."

"I'll bet it did," said Tess of the Derby Villas.

"You would have seen her begin to follow your own well-used path, and travel in a direction most undesirable to your plans. Then it was when your new gleeful scent disappeared, and your more usual scent of the fuming malady and the mendaciousness reasserted itself. Perhaps, what led the princess all the way from the graveyard to the glen was that she smelled your scent and remembered it from the brief time she knew you at the palace."

"So like her la-di-dah highness to go and leave out as important a bit of information as the fact that she followed a familiar cat's scent into the glen," said the bright and sporty assistant.

Hercules Potato nodded his head in agreement at this. "It would be natural for her to follow what was familiar now she was lost. It is when you had the luck most bad. Out of all of the places into which she might have wandered, out of all the paths through the wood that she might have taken, the Princess Anastazia, she wandered along just the path to take her to the village, to the very lane even, where lives the curiosity Blevins and the aunt of the true hero Lord Moppes."

"It would have been a stroke of luck for us if she hadn't just left that morning to go on her cruise round world," said the Colonel.

"You did what you could to disrupt what you could, did you not, *mam'zelle* MissTree?" said Hercules Potato. "You followed us on the trail of the scents. It was you, of course, who we heard rush away when we first saw the ghost dog Thane Mortimer. There you were at the scent of the fish, once more smelling of the cat in a good mood because you thought you had destroyed the royal chew toy and ruined the chances of my solving the case. You hoped that if you destroyed the royal chew toy, we would not be able to communicate with the true hero where the princess could be found. Perhaps, but I think, in the end, we could have managed without it."

"So," mused Tess of the Derby Villas, "it was a hole-and-corner business right from the word 'princess.'"

"It is all extremely irregular," said the Colonel. "It never occurred to me to consider if the case had a criminal aspect to it."

MissTree spat in his direction, and said, "C-rrrr-iminal? Is that your word for wanting one's own home back? The palace is my palace, isn't it now? Mo-rrrr-e than it can ever be for that pretentious Bo-rrrr-zoi."

"I sympathize with you, mam'zelle MissTree," said the Lady Stella. "I believe it must be a beautiful palace, but your curiosity, she is no longer there. All it can be for you without her is an empty palace, and what is the gain of an empty palace?"

MissTree purred contemptuously at this suggestion, and said, "I do not take my measu-rrrr-e of happiness from the suggestions of others. I take what happiness I want for myself."

Hercules Potato said, "You may recall, mam'zelle MissTree, my telling you about the hero philosopher Aristippus and how he might have shared with you your views on the happiness? *Mais non,* even he taught his followers to never seek happiness at the expense of another's sorrow."

"The passing of heroes and curiosities alike cause all to suffer eternal wounds," said Epimone, and Cassius concluded, "We did not know of your own such suffering, MissTree. We offer you now what comfort we can give to you, and we welcome you to make your home here in our village, in the house of the curiosity Blevins."

"It is well spoken, brother," said Epimone. "MissTree, a palace where there is no one to love you is not to be desired over a home where one lives who offers you love."

MissTree sprang back into the tree above them and said spitefully, "Cha-rrrr-ity is disgusting to me. I will neve-rrrr belong in this place, and I can neve-rrr be happy here."

Hercules Potato said, "Then you choose to be miserable. It is your own affair, *mam'zelle* MissTree."

Tess of the Derby Villas lifted her head upwards and asked the shady Tabby cat, "What was the good of your ridding the palace of the princess, even if it did succeed? The true hero Lord Moppes is allergic to cats, and he would not have let you stay there, MissTree."

Hercules Potato said, "What is important is there is now a hero reunited with his dog. As it is said by the hero bard Shakespeare, 'the cat will mew, and dog will have his day.'"

MissTree gave one last furious meow at the dogs below her, and then she disappeared from view.

"She is a perfect menace," declared Tess of the Derby Villas, "an absolute rotter, and I hope she's on her ninth life." Her expression changed as a new thought hit her. "I say, the whole adventure could have been avoided if we had just waited for the curiosity Blevins to eventually come home. She would have known who the true hero of the Borzoi was the moment she saw her."

"Regiments cannot risk waiting about for eventualities to occur, Derby Villa," said the Colonel. "Supposing she falls overboard and never returns to Dale-on-Tweedy-Down? The case had to be solved directly and with decisive action, just as it was."

Hercules Potato ran a paw through his beard and moustache, then said, "Ah well, it may be as you say, *mam'zelle* Tess, but now it is done, it is done well. Here ends the arduous case of the lost princess. She is home, and we are home. We are with our friends and our heroes, and we are happy to be free of all such things as sophist sheep, aggrieved chickens, and impossible Borzois."

AN ELAPSE of one week saw Pookie Shams officially certified as free and clear of infectious diseases, be they medieval or otherwise. It also saw Hercules Potato returned to his normal mode of impeccable appearance after having enjoyed several rounds of pampering appointments at the dog groomers.

On this particular morning, he sat on his kitchen cushion, observing with chagrin as Pookie Shams jumped incessantly, and unsuccessfully, to reach a plate of sandwiches placed on the high counter above him. A chair stood behind him, but Hercules Potato knew it would never in a million years dawn on Pookie Shams that this chair could be employed to lend tremendous assistance to his plans for mischief.

Hercules Potato closed his eyelids in an effort to shut out the maddening, illogical scene before him. Just then, the doorbell rang. The two dogs rushed as one out of the kitchen and down the hall passage towards the front door. The grand hero Gwendolyn was just opening it as they arrived at her feet.

"Why Mr. Jeffries," she greeted warmly as the petite hero Montcy came up behind her and hugged her waist.

"Hello, Mrs. Thistlewait. Hello there, miss Montcy. I hope I am not disturbing you, awfully sorry to intrude, but 'em, well, you see, I was feeling rather, well, rather like I needed to see a dog or two today to help make me feel a spot of the old cheerfulness return." He bent down and rumpled Hercules Potato's fur behind his ears. "Hello, old boy. How are you? What ho, Pookie Shams, eh?"

"It's no intrusion at all, Mr. Jefferies. In fact, we were just about to put the fellows on their leads, if you don't mind waiting just one minute."

"Of course not, how wonderful," said the hero Jefferies as he stood back up. "Time to go for walkies, eh fellows?" He smiled down on the two small, eager dogs.

They heard the grand hero Gwendolyn say, "Lewis, go and find your father and let's all go for a walk." As she returned to the front door and clicked a lead onto each of the dogs' collars, she said, "Mr. Jeffries, I had no idea you got so attached to the lost dog you found."

"I did rather," he answered, sheepishly scratching at his head. "I fell for her quite a lot, I'm afraid. I am thinking though, about getting my own dog."

"Are you indeed?" said the grand hero Gwendolyn as the rest of the family of heroes fell in behind her on the reclaimed stone pathway. "Do you think you will get a Borzoi then?"

"Oh no," laughed the hero Jeffries, "not a Borzoi, bit too much to take on in a little cottage like mine, I should think. No, but I might go in for a Labrador, much more suited to my lifestyle."

"Nothing like a Labrador for companionship," said the grand hero Gavin, deliberately not looking at his front garden as he approached the front gate. He did just stoop down to pat the soil around the crushed weigela, but Hercules Potato noted his hero could not bring himself to make eye contact with it yet.

"I think it would be a wonderful dog for you, Mr. Jefferies," agreed the grand hero Gwendolyn as the little troupe walked down the pavement along the lane.

Pookie Shams sneezed.

"Bless you," said the petite hero Montcy.

"Sneezy dogs catch sneaky rats," began the petite hero Lewis, but a quick nudge at his arm from the grand hero Gwendolyn prevented him from finishing his limerick.

Hercules Potato drew in a deep breath full of village air and marvelled at its complexity. Then, he marvelled at his perfect situation in life. He even smiled at Pookie Shams. Together, they stepped out into the kindly day, wrapped in the gracious sunshine, striding forth in the company of heroes.

~ The End ~

Alphabetical listing of French Words and Phrases

~

Ainsi que —As well
Alors —Then, or Therefore
Allons —Let's go
Attends —Wait
Attention—Be aware, take care
Au revoir—Good bye, Farewell
Bien—Good, Fine, Well
Bien sûr—Of course
Bonne journée—Good day, said when taking leave of
    someone
C'est absurd—That is absurd
C'est possible—It is possible
C'est tout—That is all
C'est vrai—It is true
Comme c'est bizarre—How bizarre, How strange
Comme d'habitude—As usual
D'accord—I agree, It is agreed
Donc—Therefore, Hence, Accordingly, So
En ce moment—At this moment, right now
Ensemble—Together
Et voilà—And there it is, And here it is

Excusez-moi—Excuse me

Finalement—Finally, at last

Incroyable—Incredible

Immédiatement—Immediately

Important/Importante—Important

Impossible—Impossible

Jamais—Never

Je suis chien—I am a dog

*Je suis enchanté de vous rencontrer—I am delighted to
    meet you*

La/Le—The

La maladie—The sickness, the disease

Le source de larmes—The source of tears

Madame—A female title of respect, or for married women.

*Mademoiselle/mam'zelle (shortened)—Miss, a girl who is
    not married*

Magnifique—Magnificent, Beautiful, Splendid

Ma fille—My girl

Ma foi—Obviously, surely, good grief

Merci—Thank you

Merveilleux—Wonderful, Great, Marvellous

Moi aussi—Me too

Mais non—But no

Monsieur—Mr., title of respect for an adult male.

N'est-ce pas?—Is it not?

Non—No

Normalement—Normally, Supposedly

Nous y allons—Let's go there

Oui—Yes

Par example—For example

Parfaitement rationnelle—Perfectly rational

Pas de deux—Dance for two

Pas encore—Not yet

Pas de tout—Not at all

Peut-être—Maybe, Perhaps
Pourquoi—Why
Quoi—What
S'il vous plait/s'il tu plaît—Please
Tête-a-tête—A private conversation between two people
Tous les deux—Both, together
Tout finit bien—All finishes well, A good ending
Très bien—Very good, Very fine, Very well
Très simple—Very simple
Un, Deux, Trois—One, Two, Three
Une promenade—A walk
Vient ici—Come here
Vite—Quick
Voila—There it is, Here it is
Vous Comprenez—You understand
Vraiment—Truly, really, very
Zut alors—Drat, darn it

~

www.ingramcontent.com/pod-product-compliance
Lightning Source LLC
Chambersburg PA
CBHW030648110726
47901CB00002B/612